WATERLOO

Bob Jenkins,
Royal Horse Artillery 1814-1817

by Bryan Perrett

■■SCHOLASTIC

While the events described and some of the characters in this book
may be based on actual historical events and real people, Bob Jenkins
is a fictional character, created by the author, and his story is
a work of fiction.

Scholastic Children's Books
Commonwealth House, 1–19 New Oxford Street,
London, WC1A 1NU, UK
A division of Scholastic Ltd
London ~ New York ~ Toronto ~ Sydney ~ Auckland
Mexico City ~ New Delhi ~ Hong Kong

Published in the UK by Scholastic Ltd, 2003

Copyright © Bryan Perrett, 2003

ISBN 0 439 97817 3

All rights reserved
Printed and bound by Nørhaven Paperback A/S, Denmark
Cover image: Detail from Portrait of the Artist by Michel-Martin Drolling,
Christie's Images Ltd
Background image: Detail from Scotland Forever by Lady Butler,
AKG London

2 4 6 8 10 9 7 5 3 1

The right of Bryan Perrett to be identified as the author of
this work has been asserted by him in accordance with the
Copyright, Designs and Patents Act, 1988.

June 1817

My name is Bob Jenkins and two years ago this month I was present at the great battle fought at Waterloo in Belgium. It was the battle that saw the final defeat of the Emperor Napoleon and resulted in his being sent to live out his days on the island of St Helena, far out in the Atlantic Ocean, where he can do no more harm.

At Waterloo I saw many of the great men on both sides, and much of what took place. I saw, too, acts of bravery that I had never thought possible, and the terrible ways in which soldiers and horses can be killed or wounded. There were moments when I was so terrified that I did not think I should survive the battle. This is my story of Waterloo, and of other things besides...

1800–1814

I was born in the year 1800. My father is head groom to Sir Desmond Holder, the squire of our village, Danesford. I have a sister called Prue, who is two years younger than me. Our house forms part of the stable block of Danesford Hall. Danesford is a large village, but not so large that one does not know everyone in it. Apart from the squire, the most important men in the village are the Reverend Mr Bell, the vicar at St Peter's church, who rides to hounds as hard as anyone in the hunt, and Dr Liversedge, who is present at the birth and death of many of us. They, and all save the few Roman Catholics and Methodists living in the village, attend morning prayer at St Peter's on Sunday. The service does not start until the squire and his family have seated themselves in their private pew at the front. Sometimes Mr Bell's sermons last over an hour and, when they do, Lady Holder raps her prayer book quite sharply on the front of the pew as a signal that he should bring them to an end. This he wisely does, as he owes his living to the squire.

As for myself, I went to the school founded by the squire's grandfather and there I learned to read and write. During harvest time there was no school, for everyone was busy bringing in the crops. I enjoyed this, especially the celebration given by the squire when all was safely gathered in. On Sundays, and at weddings, funerals and christenings, I earned a penny a time for pumping the bellows for Mr Shaw, the church organist.

When I was ten I left school and began to work as a stable lad under my father. My tasks included mucking out the stables, rubbing down and grooming the horses, fetching hay and water, polishing saddles, harnesses and brasses until they shone, and many other things. I was most interested in the harnesses for the coach and the farm wagons, and how they all fitted together. Most people talk of a horse *pulling* a cart and such, but that's not so, for the horse *pushes* into its collar, on to which the most important parts of the harness are attached. However, I must not ramble on about this, interesting as it is to me – indeed, I have been told that my principal fault lies in saying the first thing that comes into my head, and that I must curb it. I am also told that once my mind is made up about a thing, I can be stubborn.

The Holder family have lived here since Queen Elizabeth's time. A hundred years ago most of the old house, a black-and-white timber building, burned down in a terrible fire. The family built a new house on the site, but kept the old Great Hall, which was saved from the blaze. It is in the Great Hall that they give their balls and Sir Desmond, who is a magistrate, holds his court.

Father says that the Holders have always been shrewd people who have stayed out of politics, invested their money sensibly and always married to their own advantage, so that they now own not only our village and the surrounding farms, but also much else across the county. He says that Sir Desmond is a man who always looks to the future. The squire buys the latest farm machinery and is constantly carrying out what he calls "improvements" to the estate. These include drainage of the boggy areas, keeping the roads of the parish in good repair and building a bridge to replace a ford that was unusable when heavy rains swelled the river. Elsewhere, he has invested in the new canals, which carry large quantities of coal and iron across the country, and because that means more business for the coal mines and iron works, he has invested in them, too.

Sir Desmond is, therefore, a rich man, but he is also a good squire, who keeps his rents low and his tenants' property in good repair. As a magistrate he is strict but fair. For example, there was in the village a poacher called Nathan Bambridge, of whom I shall tell you more in due course. Time and again the squire sentenced him to a month's imprisonment in Dunchester gaol, but he also saw to it that Nathan's elderly widowed mother never went hungry while he was away. Finally, when Nathan would not mend his ways, Sir Desmond told him that unless he joined the Army he would send him for sentencing to a higher judge, who might have him transported to Australia. Nathan went off to be a soldier and old Mrs Bambridge was given the job of keeping the church clean and tidy, for which she received enough to feed herself and stay in her cottage.

Speaking for myself, I have always found the squire friendly and interested in whatever I was doing, but I have been warned that I must always remember the difference in our stations, for he can be terrible in his rage if any familiarity is shown towards him by his servants, farm labourers or tenants.

They say that when Sir Desmond married Lady Augusta she was a great beauty with a wild reputation. About 35 years ago they had twin boys, Ralph and Roger. Ralph was now an officer in the Royal Horse Artillery and was serving in Spain under Lord Wellington, and Roger was said to be in Australia. I had never seen either of them and, curiously, no one ever spoke of them. Then came Caroline and Sophia, who inherited their mother's looks and were much sought after by the officers of the Loamshire Militia encamped nearby. Finally, there was Tobias, who had gone off to learn the law at the University of Oxford.

Those of us who worked in the stable yard ate our dinner in the servants' hall during the afternoons. One day, at table, I asked why no one ever spoke of Master Ralph and Master Roger, and was sharply taken to task by the cook, Mrs Mason.

"It's Captain Holder and Mister Roger to you, boy!" she snapped. "And if they're not mentioned the reason is the grief and shame they've brought on the family! You'll not speak their names in my hearing again, and never in front of Sir Desmond or Lady Augusta, d'you hear?"

"Come now, Dolly, that's a bit harsh, isn't it?" said George, the coachman. "I'd agree it's best to keep a still tongue in a wise head, but nothing was ever proved, you know."

"Maybe not, but there was blood spilled and someone must answer for it, if not in this world, then the next!" said Mrs Mason, who was obviously ruffled. A little later she turned to me and I could see that she was close to tears. "I'm sorry, Bob, I shouldn't have gone at you like that. You couldn't have known, but you touched on something that grieves me so sorely I cannot even bear to think of it."

That evening, puzzled that I had caused such an upset, I asked Father what it had all been about.

"Dolly Mason loved those two boys like they were her own," he said. "She was a second mother to them. They were always in her kitchen after this and that, and it was always to her that they went with their troubles. She took it very hard when it happened."

"When what happened?" I asked, but Father remained silent as he knocked the ashes from his clay pipe into the fire.

"You'd best tell him," said Mother from her chair on the other side of the fireplace. "Better he hears the truth from you than village gossip."

9

"Very well," said Father, after a moment's thought. "But you must promise me it will go no further than these four walls."

I promised.

"Well, now, maybe you could put it all down to an accident of Nature," he began. "Ralph and Roger might be twins, but Ralph is the older by the better part of an hour, and that means that he will inherit the estate. Ralph took after his father, but Roger had a lot of his mother's wildness in him. As he grew older he got in with the bad lot at the Skull Inn, halfway between here and Brantbury. First it was wagers at cockfights, then at prizefights, then at horse races, and then it was gambling with cards. One way and another, he got into debt until he owed money all over the place. Twice Sir Desmond settled his accounts for him, but told him if it happened again he'd be cut off without a penny. It didn't seem to make much difference to him. Then, one winter's night, there was a murder in Jackdaw Wood."

Father paused for a moment as he recalled the facts.

"The dead man was a known highway robber who went by the name of Smiler Wykes, so-called because of the scar that ran from the corner of his mouth to his ear," he continued. "Smiler's body had three stab wounds in it, and when they searched the area they found a bloodstained knife and coat belonging to Ralph, clumsily hidden under the roots of a tree. Now Ralph was known to have ridden along the road through Jackdaw Wood that night, having visited the corn exchange in Dunchester during the afternoon, so things looked bad for him."

"D'you think he did it?" I asked.

"Well, I don't know. If he did, it might have been to protect his brother from the people he owed money to. Anyway, because of the relationship, Sir Desmond felt that another magistrate should investigate the case.

"I think that Ralph would have swung for it if Nathan Bambridge hadn't come forward. Nathan had been about his usual business, poaching in Jackdaw Wood, and had hidden himself in the bushes when Ralph rode by. He was positive that Ralph was wearing his caped riding-coat because it had been sleeting that afternoon, and not the bloodstained coat found later. At this stage the visiting magistrate, Mr Thornley from Abchurch, said the case was beyond him and that the Redbreasts should be called in, if Sir Desmond didn't mind paying their fee and expenses, because there were none better in the land when it came to investigating a crime."

"Who are the Redbreasts?" I asked.

"The Bow Street Runners from London, called Redbreasts on account of their red waistcoats. Two of them arrived, a Mr Robinson and a Mr Charnley, and they set to with a will, neither fearing nor caring whose feathers they ruffled. They were given a room in the house and ate with us in the servants' hall. From what they said then and by listening at keyholes when perhaps we shouldn't, we were able to piece together the way their investigation was going. Those at the corn exchange were able to confirm that Ralph had been there and what he was wearing, and an innkeeper said he had served him his dinner afterwards. Then the Redbreasts paid a visit to the Skull Inn, putting such fear into the customers that none of them came back for a week.

"Next, the Runners set about Ralph, taking turns to fire questions at him for hour after hour, hoping to break him down. They asked him if he knew Smiler Wykes, the murdered highwayman. When he said no, they replied that the drinkers in the Skull Inn had seen them talking together several times. Ralph said they were mistaken and it must have been his brother. At this the Redbreasts laughed, saying that as the two were as alike as peas in a pod, that was easy to say.

Furthermore, they went on, while he was known to have been in Dunchester during the afternoon, he had been seen in Jackdaw Wood that night, and there was no way of knowing just when Smiler had been killed. Why were Ralph's coat and hunting knife found near the scene, they asked. Ralph couldn't say. The crew at the Skull would confirm that it was the same coat he had worn whenever he met Smiler, they said. Ralph said he'd never met Smiler, so they began once more, asking the same questions again and again. In the end, they left him alone when Nathan said he'd seen Ralph ride through the wood without stopping, but you could see that they weren't satisfied."

I have always enjoyed a mystery, especially one as gruesome as this, happening on our own doorstep, so I pressed Father to tell me more.

"They turned their attention to Roger and gave him a similar going over," he said. "They told him they knew that he had big gambling debts that he couldn't settle, and that his cronies at the Skull would confirm the fact. He just shrugged and said his luck would change. They said he knew that if he didn't settle soon, some very unpleasant people would come looking for him. He said that was true, but he hoped his father would help again. Then they started to close in on him, suggesting that it would be mighty convenient for him if his brother was hanged for the murder, because he would be next in line for the estate and could borrow money against his inheritance. He protested that such an idea would never have occurred to him. They pressed him harder, saying he knew the late Smiler Wykes and had done some sort of business with him. Roger replied that he'd met Smiler once or twice in the Skull and had had a drink with him because he was amusing company, but that was the limit of their acquaintance. When they asked him where he had been on the night of Smiler's murder, he brightened up and told them he'd been drinking until the small hours with his pal, Jack Sutcliffe, known to the rest of us as Cross-Eyed Jack, and he'd drunk so much that he hadn't woken up till next midday."

"Did they believe him?"

"Hard to say," said Father, filling his pipe again. "Cross-Eyed Jack had a run-down farm just beyond Jackdaw Wood. He was a rotten farmer, always late with his rent, and was said to let his place be used for cockfighting. The Redbreasts questioned him in the servants' hall and, knowing his type, they really put him through the mangle. His eyes rolled this way and that so that you didn't know which one was looking at what, but he stuck to the same story as Roger. At one point Charnley grabbed him by the coat and banged him against the wall while Robinson shouted that being an accessory to murder was as bad as being a murderer himself, and if he didn't watch out he'd be taking the eight o' clock walk to the noose himself. I've never seen a man so scared. He scuttled out of the yard as though the devil himself was after him, and no one has seen him from that day to this."

"Was anyone arrested?"

"No, no one was ever caught. I think Mr Robinson summed it up best when the Redbreasts were taking their leave of the squire, here in the yard. 'I'm disappointed, Sir Desmond,' he said, 'because while Smiler Wykes's death was no great loss to us, murder is a dreadful crime and someone should swing for it. The fact is that as yet we do not have enough evidence to prove Mr Ralph's innocence, nor Mr Roger's guilt, though we have our own thoughts on the subject. Be assured, though, sir, that once we have a file open, it will stay open until justice is done.'"

"Was that when Mr Ralph and Mr Roger left home?" I asked.

"Well, as you can imagine, though nothing was proved, the family was unsettled and the gentry of the county gave them a wide berth for a while. The squire thought it best that the boys left home. Mr Ralph went off to the artillery cadet school in Woolwich and has ended up fighting with Lord Wellington's army in Spain. Done well by all accounts, too, as he's now a captain and commands his own troop. Sir Desmond had bought a piece of land in Australia from the government. I've heard tell it cost him little and is as big as the county. Mr Roger was packed off there with several hundred sheep and told to start producing wool on a large scale as the flock expanded. They say the squire sends him an annual payment to stay there, so that gives you some idea of what he thinks of him."

So now I knew the family secret, and you may well ask what this has to do with the Battle of Waterloo. The answer is nothing, but one result of the battle was that the mystery of Jackdaw Wood would finally be solved.

As you can imagine, our local troubles were nothing to what was taking place in the world at the time. We were at war with France, of course, and had been since long before I was born. First it was against those who had caused the Revolution there, and then against a man named Napoleon Bonaparte, who called himself Emperor of the French. Our news-sheets called him the Monster, the Tyrant and the Enslaver of Europe. We called him Boney, and Father said he would have enslaved us as well if the Royal Navy had not stopped him dead in his tracks. Now, after years of fighting, it seemed that we were winning. Lord Wellington's army had fought its way into southern France and the armies of our Austrian, Russian and Prussian allies from east Germany, were converging on Paris itself.

It must have been about 25th April in 1814 that Timothy Clerk, whose shop also serves as the post office, came running into the yard, waving a news-sheet. "Quickly! Quickly!" he shouted. "The squire must be told! Boney has surrendered! He has abdicated his throne! The war is over!"

Sir Desmond came into the yard to see what all the shouting was about. Everyone gathered round while he read the news-sheet's headlines.

BONAPARTE BEATEN AND
ABANDONS CROWN!
BONEY EXILED TO THE ISLAND OF ELBA!
EUROPE FREE FROM TYRANNY –
PEACE AT LAST!

17

There was a great hubbub of shouting and talking that stilled when the squire held up his hand to speak.

"On Sunday we shall thank Almighty God for delivering us from so great an evil," he said. "Tonight, we shall have the biggest bonfire ever. There will be ale for all and we shall roast an ox for the entire village. Mrs Mason, please take down some of your best smoked hams and make us some of the cakes and pies for which you have become famous!"

"I will, sir," she said, dropping him a curtsey.

"Three cheers for the squire!" shouted someone. They were willingly given.

"Come, everyone, there's much work to be done," he said, smiling.

Father, looking serious, took Mrs Mason aside as the group broke up. "You know, Dolly, this means that Captain Ralph will be home sooner or later."

"Aye, and so will that rogue Nathan Bambridge," she said. "They've been fighting for their King and Country, so I'll see they get a decent welcome, whatever lies in the past."

After our celebration bonfire, life in the village returned to its daily routine. The Militia went home, which upset the squire's two daughters, Miss Caroline and Miss Sophia, because they lost all their suitors at once. Early in September, while the last of the harvest was being gathered in, a letter arrived from Captain Ralph Holder, saying that he had reached England and would be granted leave of absence to return home the following month, and would be accompanied by Nathan Bambridge, who had recently been promoted to the rank of sergeant.

One frosty morning in late October I was saddling up horses for Caroline and Sophia to take their daily ride. There was a pinch of cold in the air and the leaves were turning from green to brown and gold. As the sun rose higher the autumn mist began to disperse. Glancing down the long drive I saw two riders in uniform, followed by a cart, rounding the bend.

"I think Captain Holder is here!" I shouted.

Father came running from one of the stables. The

two riders had halted for a moment, looking as though they were enjoying their first sight of home. Then they began moving forward again.

"You're right, Bob," said Father. "Run to the house and make sure everyone knows!"

By the time the horsemen had reached the front of the house, the family were waiting on the steps and all the staff, indoors and out, were lined up in our proper order. I now saw the Captain and Nathan Bambridge properly for the first time. They were wearing fur-crested helmets, blue jackets with red collar and cuffs, which were frogged across the front, white breeches and shiny black boots. Both of them were deeply tanned by the Spanish sun. I thought that they looked extremely smart. I could tell which one was the Captain because his uniform was a better cloth and there was gold lace signifying his rank above the cuffs, while Sergeant Bambridge had three stripes upon his arm.

They dismounted and the Captain shook hands with Sir Desmond, then embraced Lady Augusta and his sisters. They all stood talking and smiling for a while, then the Captain came over to the staff, greeting those he remembered like old friends. Close to, I could see that he was a handsome man, not unlike his father, with the same air of authority. Mrs Mason completely forgot herself and flung her arms round him, with tears running down her face.

"Oh, 'tis good to have you back, Master Ralph!" she cried. "You shall dine on your favourite steak and kidney pie, you see if you don't!"

"God bless you, Dolly, that is something I've thought about all the way across Portugal and Spain and into France!" he said, giving her a hug.

When it came to our turn he shook Father warmly by the hand. "It's been a long time, hasn't it, Jenkins?" he said. "I hope that you and Mrs Jenkins are both keeping well."

"We are, sir, both of us, and right glad to welcome you home," said Father, then pointed to me. "This is our son, Bob, who works alongside o' me in the yard." To my surprise, the Captain shook my hand and looked me straight in the eye, smiling.

"Then I dare say we'll be seeing a lot of each other," he said. "Bob, would you kindly see to our horses for us?"

"I will, sir, gladly," I said, touching my forelock, and ran to take the bridles from Sergeant Bambridge.

After I had finished unsaddling and rubbing down, I returned to the front of the house. Most people had dispersed to their work, but some of the inside staff had begun to unload the cart, while Father talked to

Sergeant Bambridge. All sorts of things were being taken into the house, including pictures in gilt frames, and numerous boxes and chests.

"Where did all this come from, Nathan?" asked Father.

"Spoils of war," said the Sergeant with a smile. He had removed his helmet, revealing curly black hair and a scar on one cheek. His grin gave him a devil-may-care look. "Most of it came from a place called Vittoria, where we captured the French baggage train. We'd got the French on the run by then, and they were hoping to get back to France with all the plunder they'd taken off the Spaniards. No knowing who the rightful owners are, so we got it instead. There's all sorts there – silver coffee pots, candlesticks, jewellery, and frills and fancies for the ladies, on account of many French officers having their wives and lady friends with them. Then there's those darned great pictures – as they're mostly religious, the Captain says he'll let the vicar have one for the church."

"Don't know what the vicar will say to that," said Father, rubbing his chin. "He may not be so keen on Roman Catholic pictures, you know."

"The Captain says most of them were done by famous artists, so maybe the vicar won't be so fussy when he learns their value!" replied the Sergeant, laughing.

"What about you, Nathan?" asked Father. "Didn't you bring anything home?"

"Oh, I did well enough," said the Sergeant. "Sold my share, though. Cash is more important to me, as I've got an old mother to support – and I dare say there's those at the Dog and Duck who'll not say no to a drink from me!"

During the weeks that followed, the squire gave a ball to welcome Captain Holder home. Most of the county's gentry came, although some, remembering the unsolved murder, made their excuses and stayed away. It was, however, a happy occasion in which we all shared. We saw a lot of Sergeant Bambridge at the Hall, for he had taken to walking out with Peggy Partridge, the prettiest of the maids, between whom there had been strong competition for his company. One day, over dinner in the servants' hall, he told us that now the war with Napoleon was over, the government wanted to save money and was no longer willing to support a large army.

"Our troop, being the junior, has already been reduced and may be disbanded," he said. "The Captain will probably go onto half-pay, not that that will worry him, and I'll be given my discharge before my time is up. For the moment, there's so little for us to do that we're on extended leave."

"That reminds me," said Mrs Mason. "Squire said he wanted to see you next time you called. You'd best go upstairs right away and I hope for your sake that you've not been up to your old tricks!"

The Sergeant laughed, and disappeared up the back stairs. He returned a few minutes later, smiling broadly.

"Squire says he'll have me as an under-gamekeeper when I'm discharged," he said. "It should keep me out of mischief, he says. I'm to start learning the job right away."

After that I saw a great deal of him. He told me many tales of the war in Spain and Portugal that set my imagination racing. "There was one time when the lot of us came close to being captured," he said. "On that occasion we were retreating and our job as a troop of horse artillery was to cover the withdrawal of our cavalry, which was forming a screen between the enemy and the rest of the army. Well, we left it a mite too late getting the guns hooked up to the horse teams, and before we knew it a regiment of French hussars were on us. There we were, all of us jumbled up together, hacking and slashing and banging pistols at each other, galloping hell-for-leather towards our own lines."

He pointed to the scar on his right cheek. "That was when I got this," he said. "Did for the man that gave it me, though. Gave him a good strong backhander, Cut Two we call it, right into his neck, and over he went."

"Why didn't they surround you?" I asked, puzzled. "Your horses were pulling guns and theirs weren't, so they must have been faster."

"True enough," he replied, "But would you ride across the front of a team of six, galloping flat out? You'd have been ridden down, trampled to death probably, and even if you survived that, then you've a ton and more of gun to pass over you."

"I see what you mean," I said. "But how did you manage to get away?"

"Oh, a squadron of our own light dragoons saw what was going on and turned back. The French hussars were so keen to capture us they didn't know what hit 'em when our lads charged. Chased 'em for a mile and more and came back with a score of prisoners."

I was curious about the French, whom we seemed to have fought so often, and on another occasion asked him what they were like. "Do they really eat frogs and snails?" I asked.

"Maybe they do at home," he said, grinning. "Mostly, like us, they eat what they can get. Tell you the truth, though, your average Frenchie isn't a bad sort. When we weren't fighting, we'd both live and let live, and sometimes have a chat with them between the lines. They were being paid to do a job, just like us. We both understood that, so there was no dislike. I'd say we had a respect for each other." This surprised me, as I'd been brought up to believe that most Frenchmen were fiends.

"They don't seem to fight as well as we do, though, do they?" I said. "I mean, we always seem to win, don't we?"

"Yes, we win a lot of the time," he said, thoughtfully. "But don't you go thinking that the average Frenchman isn't as brave as any of us, because he is. The trouble with them is they get excited, while we take things as they come. When they think they're winning they're very difficult to stop, but when they know they're losing they go all to pieces. I remember one captured officer talking to the Captain. 'You English are bad

26

soldiers!' he said. 'An hour ago we had won the battle, but you did not seem to understand that! You stayed where you were when you should have known better and retreated. And now look what has happened – we have lost the battle and it is we who are retreating!'" The Sergeant roared with laughter at the memory of it and we all joined in.

He had nothing but admiration for Captain Holder. "He's a good officer who looks after his men," he said. "Mind you, he'll tolerate no slackness, especially when it comes to looking after the horses, and quite right, too, because without 'em we'd be lost. When we're in action, he's cool as a cucumber – never known him to make a mistake."

After hearing all these stories, I thought that there could be no better life for me than being a soldier in the Royal Horse Artillery, where I would be given a fine, dashing uniform and be able to work with horses. When I told my parents of my ambition, one evening, they were horrified, saying that I did not understand what was involved, that I should put the idea right out of my head, and that I was too young, anyway.

As I have said, I have stubborn streak, and I refused to give in, swearing that I would run away and take the

King's shilling as soon as I could, by which I meant that I would enlist and receive a day's pay in return, which would bind me to the service.

A couple of days later I was serving as groom to Captain Holder when we visited a nearby estate for a shooting party.

"Now, Bob, I understand that you want to be a soldier," he said as we were riding home. I knew at once that my father had asked him to speak to me on the subject.

"I do, sir, and when the time is right I intend to join you," I replied.

"And when the time is right, we shall be glad to have you, if that's still how you feel," he said. "However, that time is not now. I dare say you've heard exciting tales about the war and the good times we had, but there were many bad times, too – times when you're without sleep or rest for days and nights on end, times when you're starving, freezing and wet through, and times when you see your friends killed or horribly wounded. We don't talk about them, but they happen, just the same."

"I'd be willing to take a chance, sir," I replied stubbornly, knowing that he was trying to discourage me.

"I know you would, Bob," he said, kindly. "But there is something else you should consider. The war with Napoleon is over, and it seems that we shall be signing a peace treaty with the Americans soon, so my troop is on the verge of disbandment. If you join another, you will probably spend years in barracks with nothing to do but spit and polish, and become extremely bored. That's not what you want, is it?"

I must admit that I had not thought of this, and the prospect was not one that appealed to me.

"No, sir, that's not what I want – but if we have another war, will you let me join you?"

"I doubt if we shall, but I promise to consider it," he said, laughing.

There the matter rested for a while. We had a fine Christmas and welcomed the New Year of 1815 in grand style. Time started to slip by and the seasons began to change again. Then something happened at the end of the first week in March that left us all stunned.

We were at dinner in the servants' hall when Mr Clerk walked through the door, shaking his head and looking grave.

"What's up, Tim?" asked Father. "You look like a man who's lost a guinea and found a shilling!"

"Read that!" said Mr Clerk, passing him the latest news-sheet. "Just read that – I'll say no more!"

We gathered round to read the lines printed in heavy type:

THE BEAST IS FREE!
BONAPARTE ESCAPES FROM ELBA AND
LANDS ON SOUTH COAST OF FRANCE!

For a moment we were all struck dumb.

"He'll not get far now the French have got their proper king back!" commented Mrs Mason.

"Don't be so sure, Dolly," said Sergeant Bambridge. "By all accounts, this King Louis they've got now hasn't done much to make them love him. The Captain had better be told, because somehow I think the government will have need of us."

A week later the news-sheet read:

BONEY MARCHES NORTH
THROUGH FRANCE!
TROOPS DESERT TO HIM
IN LARGE NUMBERS

The following week the news was even worse:

KING LOUIS XVIII FLEES PARIS!
THE TYRANT NAPOLEON ENTERS
FRENCH CAPITAL!
PREPARATIONS FOR WAR

That same day a soldier galloped into the yard with orders for the Captain. I knew at once that he would be off to war and approached him as soon as he appeared. "Will you take me with you, sir?" I asked. "You promised to consider it."

"So I did," he replied, then called for my parents. "Bob wants to come with me," he said to them. "What do you say?"

"I say he's too young, sir!" cried Mother, beside herself. "Please don't take him!"

"I'm fifteen now!" I retorted. "That's older than many a drummer boy who served in Spain!"

"You're not going and that's that!" shouted Father.

"You can't stop me!" I shouted back. "I'll run away!"

"That's enough!" said the Captain, sharply. "I propose that I shall take the lad, but as my servant and not as a soldier. It is better that I should be able to keep an eye on him and see that he stays out of harm's

31

way than that he should run off and get into all sorts of trouble with the wrong people."

"Maybe the Captain is right," said Father, putting his arm round Mother, who had burst into tears. "We can't lock the boy up, and anyway he's more than half way to being a man now. What's more, if he's the Captain's servant, he won't be doing any fighting." Mother, nodded, but continued to sob.

"That's settled, then," said the Captain. "Jenkins, I want you to go to Dunchester market tomorrow and buy me two good packhorses. Bob can practise packing my campaign kit on them. Sergeant Bambridge and I will be returning to the troop in the morning and I'll send for Bob as soon as I have firm orders about where we're going."

"Very well, sir," said Father.

The two horses we bought were named Horace and Virgil. They were good strong animals and used to the work they were intended for, although I thought that Horace was a mite frisky and inclined to be awkward. I looked out the Captain's campaign kit and was surprised how much of it there was. There was a tent, a collapsible bed, table, chair and washbowl, a big trunk fitted out as a wardrobe, a lamp, cooking pots, food containers, a coffee pot, cups, saucers, plates, cutlery, cleaning materials and much more besides. With Father's help I found a way of packing everything on the horses, leaving room for me to ride one of them, then practised doing it until I could do so quickly, and in the dark.

In the middle of April a soldier arrived from the Captain's troop. His name was Bill Grover and he brought word for me to join the troop in Colchester by the 25th of the month. It had been ordered to serve in the Low Countries of Belgium and the Netherlands and was due to sail there from Harwich three days later. I had been eagerly awaiting my orders, for in addition to the honour of serving with the troop I dearly wanted to see something of the world outside the village. Yet when the moment came, I found it a terrible wrench to leave home and all those I had grown up with.

When the packhorses were loaded, Mrs Mason came bustling out of her kitchen with pasties for our journey and instructions to look after the Captain properly. Mother put a brave face on it, although I could see that she had been crying. She and my sister,

Prue, both gave me a hug, telling me to come back safe and write often. Father shook my hand, which he had never done before, gave me a guinea, told me I had a responsible job to do and said he looked forward to my return. Then Bill Grover and I trotted off down the drive. I had a large lump in my throat. When we reached the bend I looked back at the Hall. They were still standing there, waving, and I waved back. Around the bend lay an unknown future, and adventures I had never dreamed of.

I think Bill Grover must have known how I felt, for we trotted along in silence for a while. When he did speak, it was in an interested, friendly manner and as we talked I began to feel better. He was 22 years of age, fair-haired and, like the Captain and Nathan Bambridge, deeply tanned from his years in Spain. It took us three days to get to Colchester, sleeping in barns at night to save money so that we could buy good meals in the inns we passed. During that time Bill told me much about my new life.

He said that the Royal Horse Artillery was the most exclusive branch of the entire Royal Regiment of Artillery, and that the competition to join it, especially among the officers, was fierce, but only the best were accepted. He explained that the difference between ourselves and the field artillery was that every member of the gun detachment was mounted, with two men sitting on the limber, which is like a two-wheeled cart with an ammunition box on top, three men driving the horse team and the rest had their own horses.

"That way," he said, "we can move fast and get into action very quickly, just where we're needed."

Our own troop, he continued, was the most junior, but every bit as good as any of the others. It was generally referred to by the name of its commander and was called Holder's Troop throughout the Army. During one of the earliest actions in Spain its first commander had been killed and Captain Holder, who was then a lieutenant, had taken over and handled the troop so well that he was confirmed in command and promoted.

"How many guns does the troop have?" I asked.

"We have six 6-pounders," said Bill. "When it was decided to raise us to full strength again, the Captain was hoping we would get 9-pounders, like some of the other troops. But there weren't enough to go round and being last on the list we had to take what we could get. We should have a howitzer as well, but we haven't." I had heard of howitzers but had no idea why they were different from guns. Bill explained.

"Well, a gun fires round shot – that's cannonballs to you – in what you might call a straight line at the target. It can also fire canister, which is simply a lot of musket balls in a tin container, turning it into a giant shotgun when the enemy gets too close for comfort. We keep both types of ammunition in the limber. Now, a howitzer works differently. It fires a shell up into the air so that it passes over a house or a hill behind which the enemy might be lurking, and bursts among them. It's a useful thing to have."

"Is what you've got in the limber the only ammunition you've got?" I asked.

"Not by a long chalk!" he replied, laughing. "Why, that wouldn't last us long in a tight corner! No, we've got six four-wheeled ammunition wagons as well that will come up to the guns as required. Very useful on the march they are, too, for we store our bread and other things in them."

When I said that the guns and ammunition wagons must occupy a lot of road when the troop was on the march, he nodded in agreement.

"Aye, and that's not all, Bob. We also have two spare gun carriages to replace those damaged in action, a forge cart so that we can do our own shoeing and so on, what we call a pioneer cart containing all manner of useful tools like spades, picks and axes, and then there's our own baggage wagons. Because we're called a troop a lot of people think that we're few in numbers, but that's not so. In fact, at full strength we have six officers and 184 men, and no less than 220 horses."

By the time we reached Colchester I knew a great deal more about the troop and how it worked, all of which was to come in useful. When we clattered through the barracks gate the first person I saw was Sergeant Bambridge, who gave me a cheery wave.

"Hello, young Bob!" he shouted. "Got your way, I hear, and now you're coming along o' us!"

But there was no time for more conversation as all was hustle and bustle, and the Sergeant was busy with his duties. Bill showed me the way to the stables, where I unloaded the horses, rubbed them down and saw to it that they had a good feed and water. The troop horses I saw were magnificent animals with shining coats, groomed to perfection. Then I went in search of Captain Holder. On the way I passed the guns, drawn up on the barrack square, their brass barrels polished so that they gleamed in the sunlight.

At length I found the Captain in an office. He and his officers were studying orders for the march to Harwich and our embarkation there. He greeted me kindly, but was brusque and businesslike at the same time.

"Ah, Bob, you've got here in good time – well done," he said. "Now this concerns you. We shall be sailing to Ostend and because the harbour is likely to be crowded we may have to swim our horses ashore on the beach outside the town. Obviously I don't want my kit soaked with seawater, so find a place for it on one of the baggage wagons until we're on the other side. Then you can pack it on the horses again. One other thing – I'd like you to stay with the horses during the voyage, because they won't like it."

"I will, sir, though I cannot swim myself," I said. I must have looked glum, for he burst out laughing.

"Don't worry, Bob – horses can swim naturally! Just hang onto something, even if it's a tail, and make sure you don't get kicked!"

May – mid-June 1815

Two days later the troop set out for Harwich. It made a grand sight as it passed through the villages, where people came out to wave and cheer, and I felt proud that I was part of it, even though I was not a soldier. At Harwich the guns and wagons were swung aboard ships while the horses were led across gangways onto what looked like large sailing barges, and tethered in stalls. I had never seen ships or the sea before, so it all seemed like a great adventure when we cast off and began to move down the river. When we reached the open sea it was calm enough, but the horses obviously did not like the rolling of the craft. They began to stamp and neigh and even their feed did not calm them. Horace bared his teeth, rolled his eyes and was so badly frightened that there was no calming him for the first few hours.

I was frightened myself when we reached Ostend two days later, for I was dreading the prospect of swimming the horses ashore. Fortunately, I had told Bill my worries. As I normally rode Virgil, he told me to saddle and ride him when the time came, leading Horace. We were anchored about 150 yards off the low shoreline, but it might as well have been a mile as far as I was concerned. I noticed that there were two lines of boats, formed into a lane to keep the horses heading in the right direction. The sailors lowered a gangway and secured it with ropes. Then the horses were taken out of their stalls in turn. At first they were reluctant to enter the water, but after the first few had plunged in and struck out for the shore, urged on by the shouts of the men in the boats, the rest followed in a steady stream. They did not have to swim far, for their hooves seemed to touch the gentle slope of the sandy seabed about 100 yards from the shore, and they waded in to be rounded up.

I was last and, as though he could read my own thoughts, Horace proved reluctant to approach the gangway. At length I got him there, mounted Virgil, and wound the leading rein round my hand. I need not have worried, for suddenly the sailors shouted and simultaneously gave both horses a mighty thwack on the rump. With a tremendous splash, Virgil plunged in. Suddenly I was up to my chest in water so cold it took my breath away. For an instant I thought I would be unseated, but I clung to the saddle for dear life. Then

I opened my eyes and saw his head surface. I felt him strike out beneath me and the water now only covered my legs. Horace was swimming alongside us, rolling the whites of his eyes and looking afraid. When we splashed ashore through the shallows I was bitterly cold and dripping with water, but had begun to feel quite pleased with myself.

The ships carrying the rest of the troop had reached Ostend ahead of us. Ashore, the gunners were forming up the teams and, under the orders of a naval officer, were being directed through the town to the quay onto which the guns and wagons were being unloaded. I found the wagon containing the Captain's kit and packed it onto the horses. Troop Sergeant Major Price, who knew who I was, told me to accompany him to a field outside the town on the Brussels road, where the troop would spend the night prior to making its next march. There he told me where to unload the horses and pitch the Captain's tent, saying that would form the troop's headquarters for the moment. While I did this and set up the Captain's bed, table, chair and washbowl, the troop's guns and wagons began to come in. The Sergeant Major told them where to go, and in a short space of time the field was covered with neat lines of guns, wagons, tethered horses and tents. Soon everyone was busy feeding and watering the horses and brushing the salt out of their coats, and I did likewise. When I had finished I went back to the Captain's tent, where the Captain had just finished giving his orders for the next day. On my way I saw that some of the gunners had lit fires and put cooking-pots on them.

"You've been busy, Bob," the Captain said. "Well done."

"I'm afraid I haven't got anything for you to eat yet, sir," I replied, feeling guilty that I had not thought of this earlier. He laughed and clapped me on the shoulder.

"Don't worry about it. In the field, officers and men rough it together and share the same rations. That way there's no ill feeling between us. In other armies the officers insist on their privileges and keep the best rations for themselves. The result is the men hate them and won't do anything unless they're ordered to. Come on, grab a plate and some cutlery and we'll see what the others have got for us."

We joined a group seated round a fire and received a good helping of rich beef stew with potatoes and vegetables, with a hunk of bread to mop up the gravy. Being ravenous, I ate heartily. Everyone seemed free and easy with each other as they chatted and joked, although due respect was paid to the Captain. This was just what I thought life in the Army was about and I thoroughly enjoyed it. Afterwards, I cleaned up our plates, found a space for myself in one of the baggage wagons, rolled myself in a blanket and was asleep before I knew it.

Next morning I was woken up by the sound of a trumpet sounding Reveille. After breakfast the troop was quickly on the road, leaving me a little alarmed as I still had to strike the Captain's tent and pack his things. He did not seem worried, saying that I should follow on along the road to Brussels, and catch up with the troop later.

Until now, I had been too busy to take much notice of my new surroundings, but as I jogged along I looked about me with interest. The country was flat with only the occasional rise, and there were many more windmills than there are at home. There were canals, too, on which I saw barges working.

I caught up with the troop at about noon, shortly before we passed through the pleasant town of Bruges. We then carried on along the Brussels road for about ten miles and again camped for the night. Next morning we passed through Ghent, and the nature of the country changed slightly, being better wooded and more gently rolling, although nowhere was there anything you could call a hill.

Finally we reached a village just west of Brussels. There, for the moment, we occupied the buildings of a school, forming horse lines and gun and wagon parks in a field opposite. Luckily for me, the Captain had a room to himself and I did not have to pitch his tent. In fact, apart from looking after Horace and Virgil, most of my duties involved keeping his uniform clean and tidy.

By now, I had become familiar with most of the troop's officers. The Captain's second-in-command was Captain Giles Mowbray, the adjutant and quartermaster was Lieutenant Jacob Burman, who was responsible for the daily administration of the troop, and Lieutenants Paul Collier, Ian Elliot and Philip Holt were each responsible for a section of two guns. As there were several more Royal Horse Artillery troops billeted in the area, and many of the officers had known each other in Spain, there were uproarious parties when they visited each other's messes.

I accompanied the Captain as his groom on several trips he made into Brussels. Infantry and cavalry regiments were camped everywhere along the road, constantly marching and drilling in the fields. I knew that British infantry wore scarlet, as did our own heavy cavalry, that our hussars and light dragoons wore blue, as did the Royal Artillery, and that our riflemen wore green, but I was bewildered by the rest of the uniforms, which were of every colour imaginable.

"Dutch-Belgian infantry," said the Captain, as we passed a regiment at drill. They wore blue coats, but I knew that the French infantry did as well and wondered how they would tell each other apart when the time came.

"Here, look at this lot," he continued, pointing at a troop of cavalry trotting towards us. "Brunswick Hussars – sinister-looking beggars, aren't they?" They were indeed, for apart from a yellow-and-blue sash and blue collars, they were dressed from head to foot in black, with silver skull-and-crossbones on the front of their headdress.

Brussels was the first big city I had ever been in. It was far larger than Dunchester, our county town, and contained many fine houses that were taller than ours, but not always so wide. It also had a big square called the Grande Place in which Dunchester Market Square would have fitted neatly into a corner. There was a cathedral, shops galore and tree-lined walks in which officers strolled with their ladies. There were men in uniform everywhere, all going about their business.

One day the Captain attended a meeting to which all commanding officers had been summoned. He emerged with a Major William Ramsay, whom I knew commanded a troop billeted not far from our own.

"The Duke is not pleased, I fear," said Major Ramsay, as they swung into their saddles.

"I fear not," replied the Captain.

As they turned for home I dropped back behind them, but stayed within earshot of their conversation. I knew that the Duke they referred to was Lord Wellington, who had been raised to that rank of the peerage in recognition of his victories in Spain, and was now a field marshal.

"He is very critical of the quality of our own troops and those of our allies and has gone so far as to say that he has been given an infamous army with which to meet Napoleon," said Ramsay.

It was not my place to comment, but this surprised me. Although I knew very little about such things, it seemed to me that with all the men and guns I had seen gathered together around Brussels, we should have no difficulty in defeating the enemy.

"You can see what he means," commented the Captain. "It would be different if we had the same army we had in Spain, but many of the experienced infantry regiments were shipped off to fight the Americans and may not return in time. Most of those we have here have not seen a shot fired in anger. They will do their best, I expect, but there's no substitute for experience. Lucky we've still got the King's German Legion."

"True, but they are much reduced in numbers," replied Ramsay. "Their infantry battalions now have only six companies apiece instead of ten."

They proceeded in thoughtful silence for a while. I had heard about the King's German Legion. The King of England is also the ruler of Hanover in Germany, and when the French had invaded that country many of his subjects had volunteered to fight for him and had been formed into their own German-speaking regiments. By all accounts they had fought well in Spain and were the only foreigners that British troops would regard as their equals.

"What about our Allies?" said the Captain at length. "Can we rely on them?"

"I don't know. Some of the Dutch-Belgians were fighting for Napoleon only a year or two ago and they will have mixed feelings. Some will fight and some won't, I expect. We'll just have to wait and see. The same goes for some of the German militia regiments that have joined us."

"Then it's just as well we have Marshal Blucher's Prussian army to the east of us. That should occupy some of Boney's attention."

Shortly after, Major Ramsay went his own way and the Captain called me forward. "Bob, did you hear what we were talking about?" he asked.

"I wasn't listening deliberately, sir, but I did hear most of it."

"Well, keep it to yourself," he said, seriously. "Everything is not as it should be, but I don't want people getting alarmed. Between ourselves, I think we've got one hell of a fight on our hands." I did as I was bidden, but found that most of the troop had already worked things out for themselves.

I usually ate my meals with Bill Grover's gun detachment, which was under the command of Sergeant Nathan Bambridge. "I don't mind fighting and taking risks, because that's what I'm paid to do," said Sergeant Bambridge at dinner that night, "But I do like to know I can rely on the folks I'm fighting alongside."

"Aye, some of this lot remind me of the Spaniards," replied Bill. "Maybe they'd turn up for a scrap, and maybe they wouldn't. And if they turned up you'd never know whether they'd fight or run. Couldn't rely on 'em."

"No discipline and bad officers, that was their trouble," said the Sergeant. "Sometimes I wished Hookey had ordered us to turn our guns on them, they were so useless."

"Who's Hookey?" I asked. They both laughed.

"Why, the Duke o' Wellington, of course, on account of his long hooked nose!" said Nathan.

A sudden thought seemed to strike him. "You know, Hookey's beaten most of Boney's marshals," he said, "But he's never fought a battle with Boney himself, and that gentleman is said to be a very tricky customer indeed."

"No point in worrying, Nat," said Bill. "There's not a darn thing any of us can do about it!"

The next time I went into Brussels with the Captain something strange happened. As usual, the pavements in the centre of the city were crowded. So common had the sight of soldiers become that usually no one paid us much attention, and I was therefore surprised to see a man and woman staring hard at us from under the trees. The woman had fashionably styled black hair and was expensively dressed, and she had the sort of dark-eyed good looks that I have heard Mother describe as "common". The man was flashy, too. He wore a grey silk top hat, a well-cut, plum-coloured coat with

49

a brocade waistcoat, and his cravat was held in place by a gold pin containing a large jewel the like of which I had never seen before. He had a wide moustache that curled upwards at the ends. It was the Captain he was staring at, and his expression was far from pleasant. The odd thing was that I thought I recognized him, but I could not remember where I had seen him before. At the time it did not seem worth mentioning the incident to the Captain.

15th – 16th June 1815

Events now followed so quickly upon each other that I must tell my story by the day, and sometimes by the hour. Rumours ran like wildfire through the ranks that Napoleon had crossed the Belgian frontier at the head of a large army and was marching towards Brussels. These seemed to be confirmed by the fact that the Duke had already despatched troops southwards as an advance guard, but no one seemed to know anything for certain. Nevertheless, Captain Holder brought the troop to a state of readiness so that it would be able to move at a moment's notice. Everyone was unsettled by the uncertainty. I wanted to see my first battle but I felt uneasy and perhaps a little afraid, although I would not be taking part in the fighting.

"What happens if one of the horses in a team is killed or badly injured?" I asked Bill. The troop's horses were such magnificent animals and I hated the idea that any of them should be hurt.

"Well, we have to cut it out of the team pretty sharpish," he replied, and showed me how the harness was ingeniously made so that the remaining horses could take the strain and get the gun moving quickly again. "I know what you're thinking," he said. "None of us like it, but they've got a job to do, just like us, or they wouldn't be here."

Later I asked the Captain whether we would be moving, as I would have to pack Horace and Virgil.

"I don't know, Bob," he said, thoughtfully. "The Duke and his staff don't seem worried. In fact, they're attending a ball given by the Duchess of Richmond tonight. I'm going myself and I'd like you to come along as groom."

The midsummer evenings were long so it was still light when we trotted into Brussels. We found the Rue de la Blanchisserie, where the Duchess had taken a house. It was lit by flaring torches and was already crowded with coaches and horses, so I had trouble finding a convenient place to tether Virgil and the Captain's mount, a fine bay mare named Rosie. Then there was nothing for me to do save wait, probably until the small hours of the morning, and talk to the other grooms, most of whom were soldiers.

At about midnight one of them, a dragoon, strolled over from the other side of the road.

"Your bloke's Captain Holder, isn't he?" he said

"Yes, that's right."

"Thought I recognized him. Worked with our regiment in Spain once or twice," he continued. "I've just had a flashy-looking cove asking after him."

I immediately remembered the man I had seen staring at us on our last visit. "Did he have a fancy waistcoat, grey silk topper and a big jewel in his cravat?" I asked.

"Yes, that's the feller. Says he was an old pal of the Captain's and wanted to look him up, but not to let on 'cos he's planning a surprise. But there was something funny about him so I didn't tell him where you're billeted."

"I wonder why he didn't come and ask me," I said.

"That's what I thought," replied the dragoon. "Anyway, he's shoved off. Might be a toff, but he's not the sort I'd have thought your bloke would keep company with. Better warn him, 'cos I think Mister Fancy Weskit is up to no good."

I wondered who the mysterious stranger was, and why was he so interested in us? He couldn't be a spy, I thought, because spies wouldn't draw attention to themselves by wearing flashy clothes. Did the Captain owe him money? I didn't think so, because as far as I knew he hadn't any debts at all. And why hadn't he made himself known earlier? I was still thinking about it when, at about a quarter past one, officers began leaving the ball in a hurry, the Captain among them.

"It's started, Bob!" he said, springing into the saddle. "Make your own way back – I've got to get the troop moving! We're heading for a place called Quatre Bras – that's a crossroads on the road to Charleroi. I'll send word for you to join us there when I get the chance!"

With that he turned Rosie's head and galloped off. As I made my way back to the billet, infantry and cavalry regiments were forming up outside their quarters and encampments and, together with artillery batteries, beginning to converge on the main road that led southwards to Charleroi. Often I was forced to halt Virgil at the side of the road as troops marched past. A Highland regiment went by with pipes skirling, a sound I had never heard before, then more British infantry, marching to the beat of the drum, then Dutch-Belgians, green-clad Nassauers, black Brunswickers, colourful hussars, dragoons, both heavy and light, and battery after battery of guns. Eventually I was able to work my way through, but the sky had already begun to lighten by the time I reached the school that was our billet.

The troop had gone. I had not passed them on the road and assumed that they had made their way forward by another route. Three of the ammunition wagons, the forge wagon, the pioneer cart, the baggage wagons and their drivers were all that were left behind. Mr Burnham was the only officer remaining. He told me that until further orders were received they would remain where they were. I suddenly felt very lonely, as almost everyone I knew had gone.

I cooked myself some breakfast, then groomed Horace and Virgil and began packing the Captain's things. Nothing happened for the rest of the morning. At about one o'clock Mr Burnham received orders to move the wagons through Brussels and down the Charleroi road to a village called Mont St Jean, to the west of which he was to establish a vehicle park. As there was not much preparation to do, we moved off shortly after.

Brussels seemed strangely deserted as we passed through. There were very few soldiers about and most of the civilians had an apprehensive look about them. The first part of the Charleroi road passed through a large area of wooded country that I learned was called the Forêt de Soignies. Shortly after we left this we passed through a substantial village called Waterloo that I little imagined at the time would give its name to the great battle. Beyond that we came to Mont St Jean, where a road forked off to the right. We took this and drew in alongside the wagons of several other troops.

We were situated some way behind a low crest along which I could see infantry and cavalry taking up position. I asked Mr Burnham why they were not marching towards Quatre Bras, where our own troop was. He said that he didn't know for certain, but he suspected that if the French couldn't be stopped at Quatre Bras, this would be a good position to fall back on.

"The Duke understands the French," he explained. "He knows they like to attack. He's a good defensive general and in Spain he used to place our main line just behind a ridge like this. The French would come on in their columns, yelling and cheering, but when they appeared over the crest our infantry would blow away their leading ranks with a couple of sharp volleys, then charge straight in with the bayonet and drive them back down the slope."

"D'you think he'll fall back here, sir?" I asked, still unsure about what was happening.

"I just don't know, Bob," he replied, shrugging. "I've been told that the French army is bigger than ours, and bigger than the Prussian army to the east of us, too, but not bigger than the two of us fighting together. So a lot depends on how Bonaparte plays the game. He may want to tackle us first, or he may want to tackle the Prussians, or he may divide his army and tackle us both together. We'll know soon enough."

I got Horace and Virgil settled in the horse lines, shared some of the drivers' dinner, then walked up to the top of the ridge to see what lay beyond. I found myself looking out over a shallow valley with a parallel ridge beyond. The Charleroi road ran in a straight line to my left over our ridge and across the valley to disappear into the distance beyond the far ridge. More troops were marching along it in the direction of Quatre Bras. On my left and at the bottom of the slope there was a farm beside the road, with a long orchard to the south of it, which I now know was called La Haye Sainte, meaning The Holy Hedge. Some distance ahead to my right front was a large country house and its outbuildings, with a formal garden and orchard to its left and wood to the south. This was the chateau of Hougoumont. Both these places would play an important part in the battle to come. Along our own ridge was a track, sunken between earth banks in places, that crossed the Brussels–Charleroi road.

From about half past two onwards I was conscious of a distant rumble to the south. It rose and fell, but became more persistent as the afternoon wore on. It sounded like a distant thunderstorm.

"Gunfire," said one of the wagon drivers who had joined me on the ridge. "Sounds as though they're hard at it down there!"

At about six o'clock a trickle of wounded men, on foot, on horseback or in wagons, began to appear. I walked over to the road to see what was happening. The trickle soon became a stream that continued to flow past in the direction of Brussels long after darkness had fallen. These were the first wounded I had seen and I was shocked by the sight. There were men with bloodied bandages about their heads, arms and legs, men with torn, blood-soaked tunics and trousers, and men staggering along supporting their exhausted comrades.

Those in the wagons, most of whom had lost an arm or a leg, were suffering cruelly, for every time the vehicles went over a bump their torn limbs were jarred horribly and they screamed or groaned in their agony. I felt useless because I was unable to help them and, sickened, went back to where the wagons were parked.

To my surprise I found Captain Mowbray there, sitting with his back against a wagon wheel, surrounded by the drivers. His left arm was hanging useless by his side and his bloodstained jacket was unbuttoned at the top where a handkerchief has been stuffed inside to staunch the flow of blood from a wound in his right shoulder. He looked pale and drawn from loss of blood but he told Mr Burnham what had taken place at Quatre Bras.

"We were holding them quite nicely, despite the fact that more and more of them kept appearing," he said. "Then some bright spark ordered us to pull back. The trouble was he directed us to use a narrow lane. At one point, between a house and a wall, it was too narrow for the guns to get through. Just then, a regiment of French lancers appeared. They must have thought they had us cold and came after us. I rounded up a few of the mounted gunners and charged them while

Captain Holder and the rest set about demolishing part of the wall. Anyway, that's when the narrowness of the lane worked in our favour, because the French could only oppose us two or three men at a time. I think that's when they discovered that the lance isn't much use in that sort of situation, because we had no difficulty in parrying them and cutting several of them down. That meant they couldn't get at us because of the riderless horses, so they began popping at us with their carbines and pistols.

"As soon as the troop was clear of the lane we galloped back. They came charging after us, but by then Ralph had a couple of guns set up and gave them a blast of canister that changed their minds."

"What happened then?" asked Mr Burnham.

"We supported a counterattack and recovered the ground we'd lost, so we've stopped their advance on Brussels dead in its tracks. The trouble is, the Prussians were also heavily engaged to the east of us, at a place called Ligny, and from what I've heard they were getting the worst of it. If they retreat, we'll have to as well, so that we can stay in contact with each other. We've lost Johnson and Cardew, and half a dozen more I've packed off to find a surgeon."

"Have you seen a surgeon yourself, Giles?"

"No, Jacob – there seemed more important things to do at the time. However, I'm not much use as I am, so I suppose I'd better."

Mr Burnham sent a gunner running to the nearest regiment to ask for the loan of their surgeon, then turned to me. "Bob, you'll find some tea in my kit. Brew a good strong cup for Captain Mowbray and put plenty of sugar in it."

The tea, gulped down eagerly, seemed to have a beneficial effect. The surgeon and his assistants arrived, their hands still bloody from treating other wounded men. He examined the lance wound in the shoulder first, wiping away the congealed blood, then dressed it with a fresh bandage.

"It is deep but clean and I shall not close it," he said. "Given time and rest it should heal from the inside, but you should avoid any exertion. Now let us look at your arm."

I had never seen a bullet wound before and was startled by the size of the bruise surrounding the hole.

"The bullet is still in there, I'm afraid," said the surgeon. "I must remove it before we proceed further. I am sorry but this will cause you considerable pain."

His two assistants took a firm grip on the wounded man, having stuffed a leather pad into his mouth and told him to bite on it. The surgeon first removed a small piece of cloth that had been driven into the wound, then probed deeply with his instruments. Captain Mowbray writhed in agony for a moment, then fainted. I began to feel sick as the probing continued. At length the surgeon extracted a blood-covered pistol ball. I was astonished that something so small could do so much damage. The surgeon continued to explore the wound, producing several white fragments that I took to be bone. With a groan, the patient came to. He looked deathly pale and exhausted.

"I must take the arm, I fear," said the surgeon. "The bone is so badly smashed it cannot be mended."

"I wish to keep the arm, even though it may be more ornament than use," whispered Captain Mowbray weakly.

"No, sir, I cannot permit that," replied the surgeon. "The danger of mortification – that is, the decay of the surrounding flesh spreading so rapidly that death will ensue – is too great a risk. I am sorry."

A table was produced from a baggage wagon and the injured man was placed upon it. I did not wish to see more, but the sound of saw grating on bone is something I shall never forget. I was told that, mercifully, Captain Mowbray fainted again, and was then placed in a wagon to be transported to a hospital in Brussels.

The sights and sounds of the day remained with me during the night, for I was awoken by troubled dreams several times before the coming of light. Knowing so little of war, I did not guess that far worse experiences were to follow.

17th June 1815

I awoke wondering what the day would bring. It seemed to me that I should once again play the role of useless spectator, and I did not like the idea. I thought that if I went forward I would find the troop and be given useful work, so after breakfast I began packing Horace and Virgil. When Mr Burnham asked me what I was doing, I told him my plan.

"Has the Captain sent for you, Bob?" he asked.

"No, sir," I replied.

"Then you'd better stay here. We've no idea of the troop's precise whereabouts, and you could easily find yourself in the hands of the French."

In my ignorance, I didn't think that was very likely. The way I saw it, my job was to look after the Captain and I couldn't do it by sitting around the baggage wagons. So, being stubborn, I argued, and although I can now see that my idea was stupid, at the time I was convinced I would be of more use if I went forward. I persisted and at length Mr Burnham became angry.

"You're a civilian, so I can't order you to stay, even

if you are behaving like a halfwit!" he shouted. "At the first sign of trouble you come straight back here, d'you understand?"

I said I would and then trotted off down the road in the direction of Quatre Bras. During the later part of the morning I encountered columns of infantry, all marching hard in the opposite direction. Their heads were down because of the sustained effort, but I could see their tired, drawn expressions and the black stains left by burned gunpowder on their hands and faces. Soon the road was so full of marching men, wagons and foot artillery batteries that I was forced off it and took to the fields. The army was obviously retreating, but from what Mr Burnham and Captain Mowbray had said the previous day I knew that it hadn't been beaten, so the Duke must have ordered it to pull back so that he could stay in touch with the Prussians. Even so, I was foolishly confident that I could find the troop as it came up the road.

I trotted on across country. After a while the traffic on the road seemed to slacken. There were, however, plenty of our cavalry about, spread across the fields in long lines. I saw a dragoon regiment nearby and, to my joy, a Royal Horse Artillery troop some way to its left. As I headed in that direction there was a trumpet call and the dragoons charged a body of French hussars that had just appeared on a low rise opposite. I felt a sudden chill of apprehension as I realized that I had reached the fighting and I knew that I must turn back as soon as I rejoined the troop.

It was too far off for me to see the details but I saw the flashing of sabres and could hear the distant shouts and yells. The French hussars must have turned tail because they were nowhere to be seen when the dragoons came whooping and hollering back, well pleased with themselves. Then they, too, formed up and began trotting off in the direction of Mont St Jean.

All this time I had been approaching the Royal Horse Artillery troop, too engrossed in what was going on to pay much attention. Dismounting, I secured Horace to Virgil by the leading rein. I walked towards the nearest gun.

"What d'you want, son?" shouted the sergeant in charge of it. "If you know what's good for you, you'll make yourself scarce!"

Suddenly I realized that I didn't recognize a single face. "I'm looking for Captain Holder's Troop, sergeant," I said, dismayed by the discovery.

"Then you're in the wrong place – this is Captain Mercer's Troop!" he snapped. "Now shove off – things round here are likely to get nasty!" He pointed towards the rise, to which the French hussars had returned in greater numbers than before. An officer, whom I took to be Captain Mercer, raised his hand and the gun teams began galloping towards the guns from the rear.

"Fire!" he shouted.

The guns went off in one thunderous roar, sending their balls into the ranks of the enemy horsemen. The gun teams were already wheeling round.

"Rear – limber up!" shouted someone. The gunners were already hooking the guns onto the limbers and the teams were being backed in. Then the whole troop was away like the wind.

"You've lost your horses, son!" shouted the sergeant as he galloped past. "Told you to shove off, didn't I?"

To my horror, I could see Horace and Virgil bolting towards the enemy. It was then that I realized how careless I had been in not pegging them down securely, for neither of them had heard a gun fired before. It had been too much for Horace's jumpy nerves and he had taken to his heels, dragging Virgil with him. My heart sank. How could I possibly return to Danesford knowing that I had lost the Captain's horses and all his campaign kit? The shame of it would be too much for me, and for my family, and I should

67

become the laughing stock of the village. Even capture by the French seemed better than that. I started to run forward after the horses, but they grew smaller and smaller as the distance opened between us. My only hope was that after their first panic had subsided, they would, sooner or later, stand and wait for me.

I reached the top of the rise just as the French hussars, some way to my left, began to move forward, keeping a respectful distance between themselves and our own cavalry. Their casualties were sitting or lying about, some obviously dead, others binding up cuts to the head and arms that our dragoons had given them. More French cavalry were riding forward in large numbers, and I could see Horace and Virgil galloping wildly between the regiments.

Knowing that I was now in the midst of the enemy army I became frightened, but what drove me on was the need to make amends for my stupidity and the belief that as a civilian I would be of no interest to them. I saw more hussars as well as lancers, dragoons in green coats and brass helmets, and cuirassiers, who were big men on big horses, wearing polished steel breastplates and backplates and helmets, as well as other types of cavalry I could not put a name to. They all rode purposefully forward, paying me little attention. Some of the men cast curious glances in my direction, probably thinking that I was a local country boy.

The sky was heavy with leaden grey clouds and it began to rain. I was now breathless and had slowed to a fast walk. For the moment, Horace and Virgil had vanished, although I was able to track them from the twin line of hoof marks. Glancing towards the road, I saw that it was now crowded with French infantry in their blue coats with white lapels. There were more infantry columns, accompanied by artillery batteries, marching towards me across the fields. It was then that another aspect of my foolishness struck me. Surrounded by the enemy as I was, how was I going to get back to our own army, even if I caught the horses?

I calculated that it must be well into the afternoon by now. As I crossed a slight rise I saw Horace and Virgil standing together between two of the advancing French columns. Both their coats were steaming heavily from their exertions, but neither of them seemed to have come to any harm, although they had bolted for more than two miles. As I ran towards them the rain became torrential. There was a sudden, intense flash of lightning, followed by a thunderclap that sounded like the crack of doom. They immediately bolted again, leaving me no alternative but to follow.

I was now soaked to the skin, hot and tired. The thunder rumbled on while livid lightning flashes illuminated the mass of the advancing French army. This time, however, Horace and Virgil had not run quite so far and after another mile I found them standing again, their flanks heaving. As I approached, Horace looked over his shoulder at me, rolling his eyes. He obviously blamed me for his troubles and had no intention of letting me catch him. He trotted off in the direction of the road, taking Virgil with him.

They passed between two infantry companies marching along the road, and into the forecourt of what I took to be an inn, where soldiers were holding a number of other horses. As I pounded after them, they barged their way among the French horses, trying to hide, I suppose. This caused a great deal of stamping and neighing, as well as angry shouts from the soldiers. When I ran into the yard I was immediately grabbed and subjected to a torrent of angry words that I did not understand.

The soldiers wore tall grenadiers' bearskin caps. They were somewhat older than I had expected, many having greying moustaches. Although I was struggling to get free I could see that the horses were of the finest quality. Most had magnificent saddlecloths edged in gold lace,

70

sometimes with an embroidered N, surrounded by a crowned wreath, in the corner.

"Let go of me!" I shouted, and broke free.

"*C'est un Anglais!*" yelled one, and suddenly they all came rushing at me. I butted one in the stomach, dodged under another's arm and kicked a third on the shins, but I was grabbed from every side and ended up with a grenadier holding me firmly by the collar. What might have happened next I do not know, for suddenly someone shouted, "*L'Empereur! Attention!*"

A number of officers in cocked hats had emerged from the inn, some of them holding what I took to be rolled maps. They were led by a man of below average height, wearing a grey greatcoat over a simple green uniform. He had dark hair brushed forward and a round face containing very intelligent eyes.

With his hands behind his back the man walked slowly towards me. To my astonishment, I realized that I was looking at Napoleon Bonaparte, the terror of Europe, the man that mothers threatened their children with if they misbehaved.

"Take your cap off in the presence of the Emperor, boy!" hissed the grenadier who was holding me. "Speak only when you are spoken to, and address him as Your Majesty!"

After the shock I had just had, it did not seem at all strange that the soldier should speak to me in my own language. By now, the Emperor was standing directly in front of me and staring into my face. When he did speak it was in abrupt bursts of French, which one of his officers translated, as he did my replies.

"Who is this I find attacking my Guard? What are you doing here?"

"I am the servant of an English officer, Your Majesty. The horses carrying his property ran away and I am only here to fetch them back."

"That is a story you might tell if you were an assassin," he said, with the ghost of a twinkle in his eye. "Have you been sent to murder me?"

"No, Your Majesty."

"No, perhaps not – not even the English would employ so small an assassin!" This caused laughter among the officers, and I felt myself going red with annoyance because he was making fun of me. "Then maybe you are a spy, hoping to discover my plans?" he continued. "If so, you have chosen a dangerous profession, young man, for we shoot spies on the spot!"

"No, Your Majesty, I am not a spy," I burst out, now afraid yet still angry. "But I shall tell the Duke of Wellington that I have seen you!"

This caused yet more laughter.

"Then you will deliver a personal message to him from me," said the Emperor, with a slight smile. "My marshals believe that he is a good general because he has beaten them. I say that he is a bad general and the English are bad soldiers! You may tell the Duke that I shall eat him and his army for breakfast!"

It was clear that he intended to let me go. I felt a great sense of relief, but I was still worried about the Captain's possessions.

"Yes, Your Majesty," I said. "May I take my horses?"

"In war, one makes mistakes," he replied sharply. "Mistakes have to paid for. You have made a mistake, and now I shall find a good use for your horses."

He began to turn away. I had no idea how I would explain their loss to the Captain, having virtually made a present of them to the enemy.

"Sir, it is wrong to keep things you have not paid for!" I heard myself blurting out. "That is dishonest!" There was a stir among the officers as my words were translated.

"Shut your mouth, boy!" said the grenadier, shaking me fiercely. I knew at once I had said too much and wondered what sort of horrible punishment would be inflicted on me. I began to feel terribly afraid as the

Emperor turned back towards me and stared into my face. To my surprise, he pinched my cheek.

"You are a rascal!" he said. "Few men would have dared to speak to me as you have done! Your master has a good servant, tell him. You may take your horses for that and one other reason. The reason is that many years from now you will tell your grandchildren that you have spoken with the Emperor Napoleon. I would not wish you to tell them he is a thief!"

"Thank you, Your Majesty!" I stammered.

"Learn from your mistake and do not repeat it," he said. He then turned and mounted a magnificent grey. One of his marshals scribbled something in a notebook, tore out the page and handed it to me. The whole entourage then galloped off. I knew that I had been in the presence of a great man, who, for all his immense power, had treated me well when I was his mercy, and I began to understand why he was able to inspire his troops to follow him anywhere. I looked at the paper I had been given but the writing meant nothing to me.

"It is your pass," said the grenadier, releasing me. "You must keep it safe until you reach your own people." The soldiers in the yard seemed greatly amused by what had taken place and were grinning at me.

"When did you last eat?" asked the grenadier. I suddenly realized I was famished and had begun to shiver inside my wet clothes.

"Not since very early this morning," I said.

"*Alors*, now you can also tell your grandchildren that you have dined with the Grenadiers of the Old Guard!" he replied, laughing. "You can tell them that no less a person than Sergeant François Dumas invited you to do so! Now come inside and we'll dry your coat."

Everyone went into the inn, where my coat was placed on the back of a chair in front of the fire. We sat down round a table and shared a meal of bread, cheese and wine. I could not understand what the soldiers were saying, although they were friendly and rather like our own soldiers, but about the same age as our older sergeants.

When I told Sergeant Dumas that he spoke English well, he shrugged and said that he had been captured during our campaign in Egypt and had had plenty of time to learn.

"Since then," he said, "I have seen much of the world. I have fought at the Battles of Austerlitz, Jena, Friedland, Wagram and many more, and I have marched to Moscow and back on these very feet."

Now that he had removed his bearskin I could see that his face was terribly scarred. He must have seen my shocked expression.

"Oh yes, I've had my share of wounds," he said. "They were given to me by Austrians, Prussians, Russians and the rest. Once, when the Tsar of Russia wanted to talk peace with the Emperor, I was a sentry outside the building in which they were meeting. They came out for a stroll in the grounds. I presented arms to them. The Emperor stopped and pointed at me. 'What do you think of men who can survive such injuries?' he said to the Tsar. 'And what do you think of men who can inflict them?' the Tsar replied. Then, just like you, I spoke out of turn. 'They're all dead!' I said, and they both laughed.

"It was shortly after that I received the *Médaille Militaire*, which is my proudest possession." He pointed to the medal pinned to the white lapel of his coat. "And now, I have fulfilled my ambition and am a Grenadier of the Old Guard," he said.

"Why do you call yourselves the Old Guard?" I asked.

"Every decent soldier in the French Army wishes to serve in the Imperial Guard," he replied. "The infantry of the Guard is divided into the Young, Middle, and Old Guards. Suitable candidates join the Young Guard.

If they distinguish themselves, they are sent to the Middle Guard. Then, if they are good enough, they join us in the Old Guard, which is the elite of the elite, the best of the best, you understand. In battle, it is always the Guard that delivers the *coup de grâce* – that is, the final crushing blow – to the enemy. This you will see for yourself tomorrow."

Suddenly I remembered that I was talking to the enemy. I said I must go, put on my coat and thanked them for the food. "*Bon chance!*" said several of the fierce-looking old soldiers round the table.

"They are wishing you good luck," said Sergeant Dumas.

"*Bon chance!*" I said, at which they all grinned.

The horses had benefited from the rest and we jogged along the road quite happily as everyone was going the same way. My coat was soon as wet as it had ever been, for it was still raining heavily, but I was obviously covering the ground more quickly than I had on the outward journey and hoped to be back at camp soon.

Many of the French were filing off the road to the right and left to take up position. From ahead I could hear sounds of firing, which I took to mean that the French advance guard was exchanging shots with our rear guard.

In the distance I could see a French battery deployed across the road, firing at something I could not quite make out. It was from this area that a trail of fire appeared, heading straight for the French battery at tremendous speed. It exploded between the wheels of one of the guns, scattering the gunners. I knew that one of the Royal Horse Artillery troops was equipped with rockets, although I had never seen one fired before. I was much impressed, but the second rocket and those that followed it were wide of the mark, changing direction frequently and without warning before exploding. Their erratic behaviour, the strange noise they made and the trails of fire seemed to upset the French, large numbers of whom dived for cover.

I had no wish to come within range of the rockets, to say nothing of what they might do to Horace's nerves, so I turned off the road to the right and tried to bypass the action. I attracted curious stares, but nothing more. Turning north again, I could see the rocket troop's horses galloping along the road until they disappeared beyond a ridge. I crossed the ridge and on the other side of the valley saw the rising ground of Mont St Jean, along which were drawn up the long scarlet lines of British infantry. It was a comforting sight, but first I had to cross the valley, in which our own men and the French skirmishers were exchanging fire. As I approached the French skirmish line an officer appeared, holding up his hand for me to stop. I showed him my pass, which he read aloud in some surprise.

"*Par l'ordre de l'Empereur*! By order of the Emperor! You have some powerful friends, young man!" He took out a white handkerchief and waved it, at the same time shouting to his own men as well as our skirmishers. "*Ne tirez pas*! Do not shoot!"

Gradually the firing ceased and I was permitted to cross the valley. On the far side I passed through a line of green riflemen, whose lieutenant also told me to stop. He had a wry, humorous face.

"What d'you mean by it, young feller, putting a stop to our little party with the people opposite?" he asked.

"I have an urgent message for the Duke of Wellington, sir," I replied. "Could you please tell me where I can find his headquarters?"

"Dashed if I know," said the lieutenant, smiling. "He didn't tell me. Never tells me anything. But if I were him I'd have chosen a nice dry billet in Waterloo village. I bet you'll find him there. There'll be a couple of sentries at the door, I expect, and a flag hanging outside. Now, d'you mind if I get on with my war?"

"No, sir, and I'm sorry if I interrupted you."

I trotted back to the road and then along it through Mont St Jean until I reached Waterloo. There, opposite a church, I saw a Union flag hanging from a pole and two sentries outside the door of a tavern. I tethered Horace and Virgil and then walked to the door, in which stood a large sergeant.

"What d'you want, sunshine?" he asked, sharply.

"I've a message from the Emperor Napoleon for the Duke of Wellington, sergeant," I said.

"Course you 'ave, son!" he replied with a rough laugh. "An' I'm the Queen o' Sheba! Now clear off before I box your ears!"

I knew it was useless to argue with such a man, so I pretended to leave, then ran at him, butting him hard in the stomach, just as I had the French grenadier. "Get after 'im!" I heard him croak as I ran into the building. I heard voices coming through a closed door and barged through it. A large number of senior officers were sitting or standing round a table. Their conversation ceased abruptly.

"What the devil?" said one of them.

The sergeant and the sentries came pounding down the corridor and grabbed me. "Sorry about this, gentlemen," said the sergeant. "He'll not try this again when I've finished with 'im! I'll..."

Before he could finish I had blurted out: "I have a message for the Duke of Wellington from the Emperor Napoleon, and I have a paper to prove it!"

"Show me," said one of the generals. I handed him my pass, which he read. "Seems genuine enough, Your Grace," he said to a man in blue coat at the head of the table. "It's signed by Nicolas Soult, who we know is now Boney's Chief of Staff."

The man in the blue coat got up and walked towards me. He had a curved nose and extremely shrewd eyes. I would describe his expression as being haughty, but not unfriendly. I knew I was looking at the Duke of Wellington. "What is the message that you bring us?" he said.

"It is not a pleasant message, sir," I said, nervously. "I do not think you will like it."

"I have never liked anything Napoleon Bonaparte has ever said or done," he replied. "Just the same, what have you to tell us?"

The room felt silent as I repeated the Emperor's comments. The Duke's face remained expressionless.

Finally, I summoned up enough courage to deliver the last and most threatening part of the message. "The Emperor says he will have you and our whole army for breakfast, sir."

To my surprise, a chuckle ran round the room, and even the Duke's face softened into a smile. "What is your name, and how came you to meet the Emperor?" he asked.

I told him my story as briefly as possible.

"Well, Bob Jenkins, let me tell you this," he said. "What you have told me is useful because it shows the enemy is over-confident. No one will have anyone for breakfast, nor yet for tea, but I shall certainly have the Emperor for dinner. He will not be able to use his artillery until the ground dries out, and by then I am assured that the Prussians will be well on their way to join us. Sergeant, the young man has done well – take him to the cook and see that he is fed and dried properly."

When I emerged from the headquarters I was sure that I had dined as well as anyone in either army. However, any satisfaction I felt at having delivered my message was blunted by the realization that I would now have to face Captain Holder's wrath for stupidly wandering off. In the gathering darkness I made my way back to the front line and found out where the troop was. As I unloaded Horace and Virgil in our horse lines I could see the campfires of both armies, although where they had found anything dry enough to burn I had no idea. At La Haye Sainte there was a huge bonfire blazing, by the light of which I could see soldiers breaking up the barn doors.

I found the officers sheltering beneath a tarpaulin slung between two ammunition wagons. As well as having fought at Quatre Bras the previous day, the troop had also formed part of the rear guard that had covered the withdrawal to Mont St Jean, so I was not surprised that they looked drawn and tired and were irritable.

"Where the devil have you been?" snapped Captain Holder as a preliminary to giving me a dressing down. When he had finished I said I was sorry and would not repeat my stupid mistake, then told him of my adventures, producing my pass, which was handed around with great interest. Finally, I told him how I had delivered the Emperor's message to the Duke. By now everyone was smiling and chuckling.

"Well, gentlemen," said the Captain, "Now that we know Bob keeps such exalted company, we shall have to watch our manners when he is about!"

It was then that I remembered to tell him about the man who had been asking about him in Brussels. When I described him the Captain said he hadn't the faintest idea who it could be.

"Probably wants to borrow money from you, Ralph," said Mr Burnham with a smile.

"Then he's out of luck, because I haven't any!" the Captain replied, laughing.

Shortly after, they made room for me and we rolled ourselves in our blankets. I lay awake, knowing that there would be a battle in the morning. I wondered what fate lay in store for me and the troop, and for those I had met during the day, including Sergeant Dumas and his Grenadiers of the Old Guard, the humorous lieutenant of the Rifles, the Emperor and the Duke. I was fearful of the unknown, but was so weary that at length I dropped into a heavy sleep of troubled dreams.

Morning, 18th June 1815

By dawn, the heavy rain had been reduced to a drizzle that slowly eased and then stopped as the morning went on. All round me men were stirring and easing their cramped limbs. Most of them had taken what rest they could in the open. Their faces were blue or grey from exposure and bore three days' growth of beard upon them, while the dye in their wet uniforms had run. We were no longer the smart army that had marched out of Brussels. From everywhere came the sound of popping as the infantry fired blank charges into the air to dry out their muskets. There was, too, the sustained hum of voices such as one hears in every great crowd. Those that had the means lit cooking fires and in this respect we were luckier than some, for the previous day one of the wagons had been back to the Forêt de Soignies to collect wood. Soon a delicious smell began to spread across the troop area.

"Can't have you fellows going into action on an empty stomach," said Mr Burnham. "I went foraging yesterday and acquired sides of bacon and some potatoes."

The gunners gathered round for helpings of fried bacon and slices of potato.

No sooner had we finished than the troop was ordered to move its guns a short distance to the position from which it would fight. I saw that it was placed between most of the Royal Horse Artillery troops on its right, and the Foot Artillery batteries on its left. The guns were sited so that they did not face directly to our front, but at 45 degrees to the left, so that their fire could reach beyond the main road and sweep across the slope.

The Captain ordered one ammunition wagon forward to refill the limbers, and sent another back to the main depot for fresh supplies. I saw Sergeant Bambridge, Bill and the rest of their detachment stowing ammunition in their limber and went down to join them.

"Now then, young Bob, there's a story going round that you spent yesterday hobnobbing with all manner of grand folks," said the Sergeant, grinning. "You're lucky not to be spending the next twenty years in the dungeons of some French castle!"

I admitted that I had been stupid.

"Well, you got away with it, that's what counts," said Bill.

Across the valley I could see the French army forming up in huge columns of infantry and brigades of cavalry. Everywhere there was a sparkle of bayonet points and a fluttering of swallow-tailed lance pennon flags. A large number of guns were being assembled into a great battery just east of the main road. Horses and men alike seemed to be having difficulty in getting the guns into position because of the mud. I pointed them out to the Sergeant.

"The Duke said that Napoleon wouldn't be able to use his artillery until the ground dried out," I said. "Is that what he means?"

"Not just that," said Sergeant Bambridge. "Cannon balls are just as dangerous after they have bounced. The harder the ground, the better they bounce. If the ground is too soft, they'll just sink in and there'll be no bounce, so the power of the shot is wasted. It will be a while to wait yet before they start firing."

Behind me, our infantry were moving into position just behind the crest of the ridge. Their colours made a fine sight. One regiment was played into the line by its band, the sound of which reminded me of the county fairs at home. Captain Holder rode up beside us, accompanied by a colonel whose face I remembered from the previous evening.

"That's Sir George Wood," said Sergeant Bambridge, nodding in the colonel's direction. "He's the Duke's senior artillery officer."

The Captain was peering at the large French battery through a telescope. "Twelve-pounders – they throw twice our weight of metal," he said, thoughtfully. "It seems they have us seriously outgunned, Sir George."

"True, Ralph," replied the colonel, "but your task is to defend our position against attack rather than engage in a duel against superior numbers."

Just then the Duke, accompanied by his staff, came riding along the line. He was wearing the same plain blue frock coat and a cocked hat. As he rode past the nearest regiment the officers saluted and I heard a voice shout from the ranks: "Good old Hookey! We'll see 'em off, sir!"

"I have no doubt of it," replied the Duke with a sardonic smile, raising his hat in the direction of the speaker. "And damn you for your insolence, sir!"

This caused much laughter. From this I gathered that the Duke was trusted and respected, though not regarded by his men with the same affection that the French had for Napoleon. This became apparent some time later when their bands struck up a stirring tune, the strains of which reached us from across the valley.

Then I saw the Emperor again, galloping along the front of his army on his magnificent grey, followed by a glittering procession of marshals and generals. I could see the French raise their shako caps on their bayonets and hear their frenzied shouts of "*Vive l'Empereur!*" As he passed each column he raised his hand, but so quickly did he ride that only those in the front could have seen him. It was a tremendous spectacle, the like of which I doubt I shall ever see again.

"It will start soon," said Captain. "Bob, you're to go back to the wagons and stay there – I don't want you to go careering about the countryside on some errand of your own."

I said that I would, but I was excited as well as fearful and wanted to see what happened. The Captain had meant me to go to the baggage wagons, which were a long way to the rear, but I chose to go to the ammunition wagons instead, which were much closer to the front. There I met Mr Burnham, who was now doing Captain Mowbray's job as well as his own, and would be responsible for keeping the troop's guns supplied with ammunition.

It was about a quarter past eleven when the great battery of guns across the valley belched smoke. A second later the sound of their discharge reached me like a roll of thunder. There was a whooshing, ripping noise as the balls came skipping over the ridge. The infantry had already been told to lie down and we did likewise, so most of the enemy fire passed overhead. However, sometimes a ball smashed into the ranks, taking off heads or limbs or smashing bodies to pulp. It was the horrible screams that nearly broke my nerve. I wanted to run and hide but suddenly my legs were like jelly.

I pressed myself into the ground, but was unable to take my eyes off the sight. The crest of the ridge at least provided our infantry with some protection but, looking to the left, I could see a Dutch-Belgian brigade positioned in the open at the point where the track crossed the main road, and the enemy's fire was knocking down whole files at a time. Our own gunners were taking cover behind their guns and limbers.

"Why don't they fire back?" I asked.

"Because we'll need all the ammunition we've got when the French attack," he replied.

A moment later I noticed movement in the French lines opposite Hougoumont. Preceded by a line of skirmishers, a heavy column of infantry was advancing towards the chateau. The skirmishers entered the wood to the south. I could see their progress from the powder smoke rising from the trees, which advanced steadily towards the buildings as our own men were pushed back. The column entered the wood and the sound of musketry rose to a storm as it approached the buildings. I noticed thin trails of smoke passing over the chateau, followed by explosions among the French, groups of whom were hurled this way and that. They broke off their attack and retired through the wood, leaving bodies strewing the ground. Beside me, Mr Burnham was chuckling. I asked him what was happening.

"That was Major Bull's Troop, on the right of our gun line," he said. "It's armed with howitzers and is firing over the buildings so that its shells burst in the middle of the French column. They hadn't bargained on that!"

I saw four companies of infantry running down the slope to reinforce the garrison of the chateau. Shortly after, the French came on again, to be repulsed once again as they tried to storm the walls. They began feeding more and more troops into this fight, and continued to do so throughout the battle, with no better result. I became so engrossed in the drama that was taking place at Hougoumont that I failed to notice that the French guns had ceased firing.

"It's the calm before the storm, Bob," said Mr Burnham. "The attack on Hougoumont was just a ruse to divert our attention, although it seems to be turning into a battle on its own account. We can expect the real attack any time now. My guess is it will take the line of the main road and try to punch a hole through our centre. Now we'll start to earn our pay."

I had overcome the worst of my fear but my mouth was dry, and I began to wonder what would happen if the French did succeed in breaking our line. There were so many of them that it seemed to me that we could never recover from such a disaster.

"The waiting is always the worst part," said Mr Burnham, reading my thoughts.

Afternoon, 18th June 1815

The sun had now come out and, apart from the fighting at Hougoumont and the skirmishers sniping at each other between the lines, most of the battlefield remained quiet for a while. At about half past one the great French battery opened fire again. Because of the crest the enemy gunners could only see the heads of our infantry, and the poor Dutch-Belgian brigade at the crossroads suffered grievously again, as did our own artillery on the forward slope of the ridge, which the French did their best to knock out. One of the troop's guns took a hit that smashed a wheel off its axle as well wounding two of the gunners. Some minutes later, Mr Collier seemed to fold in two and collapse to the ground. Simultaneously, one of the gunners was sent sprawling. The two less seriously injured men carried him to the crest. He was deathly pale, most of his left arm had gone and blood was pumping from the stump.

"Mr Collier's dead, sir!" shouted one of the men. "Nigh on cut in two! Afraid Harper here has taken a bit of a knock, too."

"Get him to a surgeon as fast as you can!" said Mr Burnham.

Suddenly Harper gave a convulsive heave. A rattling sound came from his throat, then he became limp. The gunners laid him on the ground.

"Too late, sir," said one. "He's gone."

"Pity. See to yourselves," replied Mr Burnham.

At two o'clock the French guns ceased firing. I could see why, for a dense mass of the enemy were making their way between them and forming assault columns many ranks deep at the foot of the ridge. I could see four such columns to the east of the road and a smaller force, with cuirassiers protecting its flanks, mounting an attack on the farm of La Haye Sainte. It seemed to me impossible that our flimsy line could withstand the assault of so many thousands of men. I could hear their massed drummers all beating out the same rhythm – *tum-da-rum, tum-da-rum, tum-da-rum* – continuously, and also the by-now familiar shouts of *Vive l'Empereur*!

Our troop, along with the rest of the artillery, opened fire. Now I could see why it was positioned the way it was, for its shots ploughed into the side of columns, carving lanes through the ranks and tossing men about like rag dolls. The gunners worked together like the well-practised team that they were. After each shot the barrel of the gun was sponged to clear it of the residue of burning powder, then in went the charge to be rammed home, followed by the wadding and the ball. Simultaneously, powder was sprinkled into the touchhole, the gun commander checked the aim of the gun, the portfire slow match was applied to the touchhole, and the ball was sent on its way to the enemy. Every time the gun was fired, it recoiled a little way, so it had to be repositioned for the next shot.

Such was the enthusiasm of the French that they ignored their casualties and continued to mount the slope. Then many things seemed to happen in a short space of time. At La Haye Sainte the King's German Legion garrison was forced out of the orchard and confined to the farm buildings. A battalion, sent down to reinforce it, was charged and ridden down by the cuirassiers. Next, the unfortunate Dutch-Belgian brigade near the crossroads, which had lost many men during the bombardment, broke and fled, leaving a large gap in our line. A British brigade, led by a man in a frock coat and top hat, came forward quickly to fill the gap. After the battle I learned that he was General Sir Thomas Picton, who had lost his uniform. He was shot dead but his men ran past to line a hedge and fired several volleys that mowed down the leading ranks of the French columns. Undeterred, the French fired back, causing many of our men to drop, and continued to advance. I could not see how this thin scarlet line could stand for long against the mass of blue pressing against it.

In an instant, the entire situation changed. A series of trumpet calls rang out and two of our heavy cavalry brigades passed through our ranks and charged. We all leapt to our feet, cheering. The nearest brigade swept down the slope and smashed into the cuirassiers, who counter-charged them. There was a brief struggle and then the latter broke, being ridden over as our heavies charged on, passing either side of La Haye Sainte to cut down the French infantry attacking the farm. Beyond the road our second heavy cavalry brigade, in which the grey horses and bearskins of the Scots Greys were prominent, thundered over the crest and smashed into the French columns. The nearest infantry also charged with the bayonet. I could see Highlanders, their feet barely touching the ground, clinging to the Greys' stirrups in their eagerness to get at the enemy.

The French were shattered by the charge. Their formations simply broke apart and the slopes were filled with men running for their lives from the flashing swords of our dragoons. Until then I had no idea of the terrible power of a cut from a cavalry sword, especially when delivered by a strong man from a galloping horse. I saw skulls cloven, heads lopped off and arms severed by the score. Large numbers of the enemy surrendered; others simply flung their muskets away so that they could run faster. One of the Greys came trotting back, as did one of the Royal Dragoons, both carrying captured Eagles, which were colours topped by a golden eagle, presented to French regiments by the Emperor himself. A tremendous cheer greeted their arrival.

"They're going too far!" said Mr Burnham suddenly. "My God, why doesn't someone sound the Recall?"

Many of our horsemen, carried away by the fury of the charge, had reached the enemy battery. I could see that they were not only cutting down the gunners, but also cutting the traces and harnesses of the horse teams and, to my horror, slashing at the horses' hamstrings. A lancer and two cuirassier regiments emerged at the gallop from the main French line. Too late, our dragoons realized their terrible danger. They turned for home but their horses, already blown by the charge, were tired and too slow to clear the clinging mud at the bottom of the valley. The French were on them quickly, spearing men and horses. A few managed to fight their way through, and more survivors were rescued by a charge of our light dragoons. I think about half of the two brigades came back, some riding double, followed by many loose horses, most of them terribly wounded.

"Well," said Mr Burnham, "That's put paid to Boney's plan for an easy win. Pity it cost us so many of our cavalry, because he's got far more than we have."

He turned and waved to the Sergeant Major, who was standing with the ammunition wagons some way behind us. A wagon immediately came forward and went down to the troop. Having conveniently forgotten the Captain's instructions to stay out of harm's way, I went down with it and helped to refill the limbers with round shot. Sergeant Bambridge and Bill told me that their gun had fired over 30 rounds and that the others had done likewise. The officers, having examined the damaged gun, decided that the carriage was beyond repair and sent the Sergeant Major back to bring up one of the spares. When it arrived, it took many hands to transfer the heavy barrel and secure it. While this was taking place I looked round to see what was happening elsewhere.

French mortar shells were bursting among the buildings of Hougoumont chateau, which were now blazing and once more under heavy attack. The enemy had also resumed their attacks on La Haye Sainte, with a similar lack of success. To the east of the road, they had reformed and were advancing once more. Now, however, their numbers were far fewer and they lacked their former enthusiasm. Our infantry waited until they were well within range, then gave them two volleys, at which they turned and ran again.

I believe that the time was now about three o'clock. The large French battery opened fire again, and although it now had fewer guns in action, its aim was more accurate. I went back to the crest of the ridge with Mr Burnham and lay down. The nearby infantry regiment had already lost a number of men when the Duke and his aides trotted up, completely disregarding the danger from the flying balls. The Duke told the commanding officer to retire his men for thirty paces and lie down for their own protection. He then rode on to give similar instructions to neighbouring regiments.

Our own troop, like the rest of the artillery, was taking a terrible pounding. During the next hour the recently repaired gun was disabled again and the carriage of a second gun smashed, as was the wheel of one of the limbers. Casualties around the guns began to mount. The dead were moved to one side while the wounded limped or were helped to the rear. The horrors of the battlefield had come so thick and fast upon me that I felt I was part of some dreadful dream from which I could not wake. My senses were somehow deadened, but my fear remained and I had begun to doubt whether I would survive. I saw Mr Holt walking towards us, leaving a trail of blood. His right hand had been shot off.

"If you find it, let me know!" he said with apparent unconcern as he passed us on his way to the surgeon. Mr Burnham, however, would not let him proceed further until he had tied a cord tightly round the arm. "This will reduce the flow of blood," he said. "Keep the arm raised as much as you can and loosen the cord every twenty minutes to avoid mortification."

Down in the valley I could see masses of French cavalry beginning to form up. At that moment Sir George Wood rode up and spoke hurriedly to Mr Burnham before galloping on to the next troop.

"We are about to be attacked by the enemy's cavalry, Bob," said Mr Burnham. "I must bring up the

100

gun teams because the Duke's orders are that the limbers should be withdrawn to the rear. It would help if you would run and tell Captain Holder that the Duke also orders that the guns shall fire until the last possible minute. The detachments will then seek cover in the infantry squares, taking with them their sponges and rammers and one wheel from each gun to prevent its being towed away. I shall tell him myself when I come up, but he should know at once."

As I ran past the nearest infantry regiment, the 110th Foot, its colonel, who was mounted and peering through his telescope, gave the order: "Form square! Prepare to receive cavalry!" I saw then what Mr Burnham meant, for the regiment's companies, which were deployed in line, quickly ran to form a square four ranks deep around the colonel and its colours. Each side of the square presented a hedge of bristling bayonets that no horseman could possibly penetrate.

The Captain was less than pleased to see me when I reached the guns. "What are you doing here?" he snapped. "This is the second time I've seen you in the gun position. I told you to stay with the wagons. Why don't you?"

I was suddenly very angry. I had seen good men killed and horribly injured and, although I was still

101

afraid, I could no longer stand by and watch. Once more, I became stubborn.

"Because I don't want to, sir!" I heard myself shouting. "I've got to do something and not leave it to everyone else! I'll carry ammunition or help anyway I can – and I've got an urgent message from Mr Burnham, sir!"

He looked at me curiously while I delivered the message, then shrugged. "Very well, Bob," he said. "You can help the gunners unload the contents of the limbers and stack them behind the guns."

Hardly had we finished this task than Mr Burnham arrived with the teams. As the limbers were driven off I heard him repeat the orders I had passed on. The Captain was clearly scornful about removing one wheel from each gun.

"What? Bowl them about like boys with their hoops at a fair?" he retorted. "I'm damned if we will, Jacob, for if it comes to that the guns are as good as lost anyway! No, no, removal of the rammers will suffice!"

He looked across the valley, where the French cavalry were still ordering their ranks, then turned towards the guns. "Load ball over canister!"

In response to the order the four gun detachments inserted a round of canister shot after the powder charge, then a ball was rammed home.

"I shall order you to fire at 60 yards," he continued, then pointed to the crest. "You will then run to the 110th's square, taking your rammers with you – and if any man forgets his rammer I shall personally ram it down his throat!"

"They're moving, sir!" called Sergeant Bambridge.

Sure enough, the enemy cavalry was beginning its attack. The great mass passed between Hougoumont and La Haye Sainte, fire from both of which emptied a few saddles. From my position beside Sergeant Bambridge's gun I could see lancers and cuirassiers, but it was the latter that caught my attention. With their long swords, steel breastplates and helmets they looked just like the knights of olden times that I had seen in picture books. They climbed the slope at a steady trot that never increased. The drumming of thousands of hooves became louder and louder until the ground seemed to shake. The detachments were standing beside their guns, portfires at the ready. The moving wall of horsemen was within 200 yards of us, then 100 yards, then 75 yards and closing.

"Fire!" yelled the Captain. The four guns went off as one, followed by the rest of the guns on the ridge. The round shot carved deep lanes into the enemy ranks, but it was the deadly cones of canister that caused most damage. Whole lines of men and horses went down in screaming, writhing, kicking heaps, as though a scythe had passed through them. I stood transfixed by the sight.

"Come on, you young fool – run!" shouted Bill, grabbing me by the collar. We ran for dear life over the crest, where the 110th opened a corner of the square to let us in. The two outer ranks of the infantry were kneeling, bayonets pointing outwards with the butts of their muskets on the ground, while the two inner ranks were making ready to fire. The cuirassiers, now disordered after having to pick their way over their fallen comrades and their mounts, came over the crest, clearly intent on vengeance.

"Third rank – fire!" shouted the colonel.

There was a blast of smoke and flame as the forward face of the square opened fire. The sound of the musket balls striking the enemy's breastplates reminded me of hail hitting a window. Some glanced off, but others penetrated.

"Rear rank – fire!"

More men and horses went down. The cuirassiers parted to pass either side of the square and received yet more volleys as they did so, then began hacking uselessly at the hedge of bayonets. Some pulled pistols and shot at the square, but any gaps they created were instantly filled. Now they had lost all formation and were riding in every direction. Some rode on into our rear areas in search of easier prey. I noticed that whenever a cuirassier's horse was killed, he would unbuckle his armour and run back the way he had come. At first, I had been fearful that the square would cave in under the pressure of so many horsemen, but my confidence grew when I saw that they were being held at bay. The infantry sergeants went calmly about their business, keeping the ranks straight with their pikes and pushing men into gaps.

The interior became hot and sulphurous because of the constant firing of muskets. At times the smoke hung so heavy that I could not see ten yards. Then a trumpet call signalled a counter-charge by our own dragoons into the disorganized French, who were bundled off the ridge with yet more casualties. Emerging from the square, we ran to the guns and fired into their retreating backs. Hardly had they gone than their artillery opened up on us again.

I do not remember how many times the French cavalry attacked us that afternoon. Some say ten, some twelve, but in my memory they all blur together. The sequence of events was always the same. Every time they attacked it was more difficult for them because the slopes became covered with dead men and horses, over which they had to pick their way. Every time, we met them with a blast of canister and ball, further thinning their ranks, then ran to the shelter of the square.

The 110th suffered severely during the bombardments and actually welcomed the cavalry attacks as a relief from them, but their square became smaller and was ringed by their dead. Their wounded had been dragged into the interior, which was very crowded. Once the enemy had become disorganized, our own cavalry would charge and send them packing and we would return to the guns.

I believe that we were attacked by almost every type of cavalry in the Emperor's army, including more cuirassiers, lancers, gaily dressed hussars, dragoons, horse grenadiers in their towering bearskins, and once by carabiniers, big men in brass breastplates and helmets topped with a large red plume. None of them made any impression on our square and I became very proud of our patient, stolid infantrymen with their smoke-blackened faces and wry humour.

I remember several incidents that took place during that long, agonizing afternoon. I had attached myself to Sergeant Bambridge's gun detachment, fetching and carrying ammunition. After we had repelled one attack the Sergeant began laughing heartily to himself.

"What's so funny, Nat?" asked Bill. "I reckon we could all do with a chuckle or two."

"They could have spared themselves a lot of grief if only they'd brought a bag o' nails with 'em!" replied the Sergeant, pointing at the retreating backs of the enemy.

"Aye, and a good hammer!" said Bill, who also started laughing. Soon all the gun detachments were roaring with laughter.

"What do you mean?" I asked, bewildered.

"Why, if they'd spiked the touchholes of our guns with nails, then we wouldn't be able to fire them!" said the Sergeant.

"Takes a gunner to think o' that!" added Bill. "No dozy cavalryman would have!"

At this everyone, including the Captain, laughed even more uproariously. Perhaps it does not seem so funny now, but at the time horrible sights and sounds surrounded us and laughter had become precious, so I joined in. I laughed and laughed until the tears ran down my cheeks, and felt better for it afterwards.

I remember also that during a lull Mr Burnham and the Sergeant Major brought down two limbers so that we could replenish our ammunition. At that moment the bombardment started again, killing several horses in the teams and wrecking one of the limbers. The enemy guns were taking a steady toll of us. One of Mr Elliot's two guns was struck with a tremendous clang on the barrel and was flung back on top of him, smashing his thigh. Shortly after he was carried off, his second gun lurched drunkenly to one side, its axle smashed.

It was during one of the last attacks that the Captain was wounded. Most of the enemy cavalry had gone and we had run from the square to the guns. At that moment several lancers, evidently separated from their regiment, came spurring down the ridge. Most were only too eager to reach their own lines, but one ran his lance into the Captain's back, sending him to the ground. He would have finished him off, but the Captain rolled to one side and all he received was a gash in the thigh. The lancer was for trying another thrust, but by now I had grabbed a rammer, with which I struck him hard on the head. He toppled from the saddle and was finished off by Sergeant Bambridge and Bill with their swords.

We propped the Captain against the wheel of a wrecked limber and bound up his wounds. He was in great pain and spoke with difficulty, telling me to fetch

Mr Burnham and inform him that he was now in command of the troop. I did so, and Mr Burnham ordered the Captain to be carried back to the square. The battle continued with the result that by the time the last attack had been repulsed, only Sergeant Bambridge's gun remained available to us.

There was now a lull during which I was able to see what was happening elsewhere on the battlefield. Hougoumont was still holding out, although some of the chateau's burning buildings had collapsed in ruin. La Haye Sainte was also still under attack, but from the east came the sound of heavy gunfire, which suggested that the Prussians had now joined in the battle. Some of the guns from the enemy's large battery seemed to have been withdrawn and were heading in that direction. To our front the French cavalry, now much reduced in size, were licking their wounds and showing no signs of wishing to renew the contest. I had lost all track of time but the position of the sun showed that it was early evening. Nothing happened for a while and I asked Mr Burnham if we had won the battle.

"It looks promising, but it's too early to say," he said, shaking his head. "In this business one must always expect the unexpected."

Shortly after, yet another attack was mounted on La Haye Sainte. The garrison's fire seemed to dwindle and die away, then some of them began to emerge from the farm and run up the slope towards our main line. Later I learned that their ammunition ran out at this critical moment, and that very few of those brave Germans, who had repulsed every attack on the farm throughout the day, succeeded in reaching the safety of the ridge. The French at once galloped a battery of guns up to the farm and opened fire on the troops positioned at the crossroads. At the same time one of their remaining cuirassier regiments moved forward towards the buildings. I watched in horror as one of our regiments, sent down to recapture the farm, was charged by the cuirassiers and cut to pieces in a minute.

Coupled with the close-range fire of the French guns, this seemed to be too much for the remaining Dutch-Belgian and German regiments at the crossroads. Some retreated a considerable distance while others, cavalry as well as infantry, turned in headlong flight, leaving a huge gap in the very centre of our line. A few minutes earlier, I had thought that we had won the battle; now we were in mortal danger of losing it.

To my surprise, the enemy did nothing to take advantage of the hole they had punched in our line, although they continued to make ferocious attacks on Hougoumont. At length, one of the Duke's aides galloped up and told Mr Burnham to move the troop to a position near the crossroads.

"We have only one gun left, sir," said Mr Burnham.

"That will have to do, sir," replied the aide. "One is better than none."

Mr Burnham told Bill to go to the rear, taking me with him, and bring up a good team and limber. To our horror, we found that the French cavalry had wreaked havoc among our beautiful horses, hamstringing some and cutting others across the head and neck. So disgusted was I at what had been done, that for a while I was possessed by a burning hatred of the French.

Some of our drivers had died defending the horses, but those who survived helped us assemble a team from the best ones remaining. We found an undamaged limber, refilled it from others nearby, and put in the team. Neither our drive to the gun position, where we attached the gun, nor to the crossroads, was easy. The bodies of men and horses lay everywhere and it was difficult to avoid the many groaning wounded in our path. When we reached the crossroads we were instructed by a general to engage the French battery that had moved up close to La Haye Sainte. Some of our riflemen were at work picking off their gun detachments under the direction of the cheerful lieutenant I had met when I re-entered our own lines the previous day. We also sent a few balls at our opponents, who seemed to have lost heart and barely returned our fire.

Gradually, the gap in our line was closed as the Duke ordered troops and guns from our left and right to fill it. Still the French made no move. The fighting at Hougoumont continued and the thunder of battle to the east indicated that the Prussians had now entered the fray in large numbers.

"Hm, we seem to have got away with it," murmured Mr Burnham to himself. For a little while, my spirits began to rise. Then, at about half past seven, I heard the strains of a distant but stirring march. A large column was crossing the crest of the ridge opposite and coming straight along the road towards us. The entire French army seemed to be cheering.

Mr Burnham, grim-faced, was watching the column through his telescope. He let me borrow the instrument for a moment. Behind a huge band I could see the Emperor on his grey horse, leading forward battalion after battalion among which the nodding bearskins of grenadiers were prominent. As I realized that I was looking at the infantry of the Imperial Guard, an icy trickle of fear ran down my spine. I remembered what the old grenadier sergeant had said: "It is always the Guard that delivers the final crushing blow." Did this mean that the French had succeeded in holding off the Prussians? Were they coming to finish us off?

As soon as the French column came within range, we joined the rest of our artillery in opening fire on it. We could see men fall, but the Guard marched remorselessly on. The band turned off the road, as did the Emperor, who took the salute as the battalions marched past. Three battalions remained on the road beside him, but the remainder swung diagonally to the left before they reached La Haye Sainte and began to advance up the slope in smaller columns between the farm and Hougoumont. I wondered why they had not chosen to advance straight up the road, for it would have been difficult to halt them at the crossroads. Instead, they had preferred a difficult route that was already churned to mud by the afternoon's cavalry attacks and covered with the bodies of men and horses.

Frenchmen whom we had previously thought defeated joined the columns, filling the air with their shouts of "*Vive l'Empereur*!" Afterwards, prisoners told me that the attack was made by the Grenadiers and Chasseurs of the Middle Guard. It was a sight I shall never forget, and I could understand why the very appearance of the Guard struck terror into so many of its enemies, for it came on heedless of the great gaps being torn in its ranks by artillery. Its columns passed through our old gun line and I could see the gunners running for the crest.

I looked along the ridge. All our infantry, now deployed in line, were lying down behind the crest. In the distance I could the Duke and his mounted staff, watching the French with apparent unconcern. As the enemy reached the summit of the ridge I saw the Duke turn and give an order. Our infantry immediately rose to their feet and fired one precise volley after another into the columns, shooting down the leading ranks. Those behind tried to reply, but only those in front could use their muskets and they could not match the sustained firing of the long scarlet ranks to their front.

The scene became obscured by clouds of powder smoke as the titanic struggle continued. I held my breath, knowing somehow that the outcome of the entire battle depended upon the result. To my right, a Dutch horse battery swung out of the line and began to fire canister into the enemy's flank, cutting down men by the score. Through a gap in the smoke I saw that one of our infantry regiments had wheeled forward and was doing similar execution on the opposite flank of the attack. The enemy showed signs of wavering, and at that point our infantry gave a cheer and charged them with the bayonet.

Suddenly, the Guard broke and fled down the slope. I heard a great cry of despair rise from the French army. It was as though the Guard had represented their last chance of winning, and now that it had been beaten they had lost all hope. The sight was another I shall never forget. Entire French infantry regiments disintegrated and ran, flinging away muskets and packs while our cavalry galloped through the running mob, cutting down everyone in their path, and the enemy's gunners tried vainly to get their guns away. La Haye Sainte was abandoned. On the ridge I saw the Duke raise his hat to signal the advance and the whole Allied army began pouring down the slope.

In the valley, the three remaining battalions of the Guard had formed squares. The Emperor sought refuge in one of them, but the remnants of the Guard cavalry fought their way through the fugitives and hurried him away. Our own cavalry began swirling round them but quickly set off after the running mob when saddles were emptied by several volleys. The squares then began exchanging fire with our infantry as they arrived, retreating step by step but growing smaller by the minute as guardsmen fell dead or wounded.

Along with several other guns we were ordered down from the crossroads, taking up position behind the infantry, and were told to load canister by a general. He commanded the infantry to cease firing, then trotted towards the nearest square, his hand raised. The French also ceased firing and, although a tumult continued to rage across the valley, there was complete silence on our part of the battlefield.

"You have done more than enough to satisfy honour," called the general to a senior French officer. "To prevent further loss of life, I suggest that the moment has come when you may lay down your arms."

The Frenchman replied with what sounded like an oath, at which the general shrugged sadly, turned away and commanded the infantry to wheel back, leaving our guns pointing directly at the square. Not one of those old warriors, their faces defiant beneath the brass plates of their bearskins, tried to escape the grim fate that awaited them. To my horror, I saw Sergeant François Dumas among those grouped around their Eagle, muskets held at the ready. This was the man who had shared his bread and cheese with me the previous afternoon and it was impossible for me to regard him as an enemy. I had seen so many men killed and terribly wounded during the day that I saw no further point in inflicting more death and wounds now that the battle was won. I desperately wanted it all to stop and would have cried out if someone had not given the order to fire. The guns went off at once in a tremendous blast. When the smoke cleared, the square had crumpled to heaps of men, many of whom were groaning and writhing in their agony. One tried to raise the Eagle, but the effort was too much for him and it fell on top of him as he sank to his knees.

Looking to be the first to seize the Eagle, many of the infantry rushed forward. I went forward, too, hoping that I could in some way help Sergeant Dumas. I found him lying beneath two dead Guardsmen, whom I pulled off him. He had been hit several times in the body. As he looked up at me I saw recognition in his eyes.

"*Ah, le petit Anglais*," he said in little more than a whisper. "I did not expect to see you again." As he beckoned me to come closer I could see that his strength was failing fast. "Take my medal," he said. "It is better that you have it than it should be taken from me by some Belgian peasant and sold for a few *sous*."

"I'll send it to your family if you'll tell me where they live," I said.

"These men, the Guard, they are my family," he said. "Now they have gone, there is no one left. Soon I shall join them."

As I unpinned his medal he gripped my sleeve. His words came slowly but his gaze was fiercely fixed on me. "You will show my medal to many people. Always tell them that Sergeant François Dumas lived and died a good soldier. Promise me. Promise."

"I promise."

With that he released my sleeve and lay back. He seemed to take several deep breaths, his eyes became glazed, and I knew that he had gone.

"Bob, you've been a great help but there's nothing more you can do here," said Mr Burnham when I returned to the gun. "You're Captain Holder's man, and your responsibility is to him now. It will take days to clear all the wounded from this butcher's yard, so do your best to get him into a hospital in Brussels as quickly as you can."

I thanked him, caught one of the many loose horses that were standing about, and rode back over the ridge. On the way I passed some infantry I had not seen before, with different colours and uniforms. They wore black oilskin covers to protect their shakos from the weather and were splattered with mud from their hard march. I took them to be Prussians, for they exchanged cheerful greetings with our men of the King's German Legion. I rode to the area where the baggage wagons were parked, some distance behind our original line. Once I had found Horace and Virgil, who seemed pleased to see me, I returned to the position we had held for most of the day.

It was a dismal sight. Our smashed guns and limbers lay deserted in front of what had been the 110th Regiment's square, the outline of which was clearly marked by its dead and ringed by the carcasses of French cavalry horses. Inside the square, troop Sergeant Major Price and some of the drivers were doing their best for the wounded. Those who could walk they had sent off, and those who could not were being placed on two sound limbers to be carried to the nearest surgeon. For some there was clearly no hope and, having been made as comfortable as possible, they were left to die in peace.

I found the Captain where we had left him. He was semi-conscious but seemed to recognize me. The Sergeant Major was wondering what to do about him as it was obvious that he could not ride or walk because of the great gash in his leg, while to place him on a jolting limber might reopen the deep wound in his back. However, I had once seen a picture of a litter carried by two horses, and suggested to the Sergeant Major that we should rig one between Horace and Virgil, using a tarpaulin from one of the ammunition wagons, poles, rope and harness, as this would reduce the amount of jolting. He agreed and with the help of the drivers we produced something in which the Captain could lie as comfortably as possible on his side.

Once he had been lifted into the litter, I set off up the road to Brussels. I passed hundreds of men waiting patiently for treatment at the dressing stations, outside which there were growing piles of limbs. There were groups of dejected prisoners sitting under guard at the roadside and everywhere there were soldiers wandering about. Some, I suspected, had fled the battle, and others I could see were simply looting the dead.

It was dark when I reached the city, where the citizens had begun to celebrate the first news of our victory. A staff officer directed me to a church that was being used as an emergency hospital. There were rows and rows of straw mattresses on the floor, with nuns moving between the patients. Two orderlies helped me to carry the Captain inside and place him on a mattress near the door. By now he was mumbling to himself and quite unaware of what was happening. This was a blessing, for when a surgeon with bloody hands arrived he stitched the leg roughly, briefly examined the wound in the Captain's back and told a nun to change the bandage. While he worked I asked him if the Captain would live. He simply shrugged and went on to the next patient.

There was nothing more I could do. I did not want to return to the battlefield and, having relieved Horace and Virgil of the litter, decided to go to the Forêt de Soignies. There, among the trees, I found a quiet spot where I made a little camp for myself, wanting to be alone for a while. By now I was completely exhausted. I was also famished, but fell asleep while eating some of the Captain's supply of potted meat and did not awake until long after the sun had risen.

19th June – 31st August 1815

The following day I went back to what was left of the troop and told Mr Burnham where I had taken Captain Holder. I visited the hospital regularly. The Captain was conscious again, but in great pain and terribly weak. I wished that I could do more for him, as the place was horribly crowded and stank of blood and human waste. They were still bringing in wounded men for days after the fighting, and the only reason that room could be found for them was that many of those already present were being carried out, dead.

I spent most of my time bringing clean laundry for the Captain, buying such things as he needed, and looking round Brussels. The hospital was usually quieter in the evening, when the surgeons, orderlies and nuns took their meal, so I took to visiting then. One evening, to my horror, I found two civilian roughs trying to smother the Captain with a pillow. I rushed at one of them, knocking him over, and shouted for help as loud as I could. The orderlies came running and there was a bit of a tussle. I am sorry to say that the roughs succeeded in breaking free. We chased them into the street, but they were too fast for us and managed to escape. As we were walking back I spotted the flashy-looking man I had seen earlier, standing near the hospital. He glanced at me, then turned quickly away and disappeared round a corner.

I felt a sudden chill run down my spine, for I was sure that this mysterious individual was somehow connected with the incident, although the orderlies told me that there were plenty in the city who were not above robbing a wounded man. Fortunately, the Captain had come to no harm, although he was shaken by the ordeal.

One evening Mr Burnham visited the hospital, bringing both bad and good news. Captain Mowbray's wound had festered and he had died of a fever, but Mr Holt had survived the loss of his hand and Mr Elliot's thigh had been set satisfactorily, although it was thought that he would always walk with a limp.

"The sad thing is, Ralph, that the troop has been disbanded," said Mr Burnham. "One way or another, we'd lost half the men and half the horses. I've had to send the rest on to reinforce other troops who've been badly hit, and I'm only staying behind to tidy up and see that our wounded are properly looked after."

The Captain nodded resignedly. I knew that the troop had been his pride and joy, and the news must have hurt him deeply. Mr Burnham obviously understood how he was feeling.

"I doubt if they would have needed us much longer anyway," he said. "The word is that Boney has been chased out of Paris and has abdicated for the second time. It's only a matter of time before he's caught or hands himself over, then there'll be no more work for us to do."

I saw his expression change as a sudden thought struck him. "By the way, Ralph, someone's been asking for you," he continued. "Natty dresser. Came to see us a couple of days after the battle. Wanted to know whether you'd survived. Bob had already told me you were here and he said he'd call in."

"I've already had a couple of unwelcome visitors," replied the Captain. "Can't say I'd be pleased to see them again."

When Mr Burnham asked him what he meant I told him about the two roughs we'd frightened off and the man who seemed to be dogging our footsteps.

"It looks as though someone's got it in for you, Ralph," he said.

"I can't think who – so far as I know I haven't any enemies."

"Just the same, I think I'll arrange for you to be moved. There's no way of keeping track on who enters and leaves this place," said Mr Burnham.

Next morning the Captain was transferred to the home of a civilian doctor. There, given proper treatment and nursing, he began to recover quickly. One day, at the beginning of August, I was pleased to find him sitting up in a chair with an atlas on his knee and a pile of newspapers beside him.

"Well, Bob, that's that," he said cheerfully. "It seems that Boney has handed himself over to us, after all, and we've packed him off to an island called St Helena in the South Atlantic. It's so small I had trouble finding it on the map."

"He won't find it so easy to escape from there, sir," I said, looking at the speck on the map, surrounded by hundreds of miles of sea in every direction.

"No, he won't, so in the end it's been worth it, although we've all lost many good friends in bringing it about. I'm told the Duke said that the only thing sadder than a battle won is a battle lost, and I agree with him."

Two weeks later the Captain's health had improved so much that the doctor had told him he would soon be fit to travel.

"I'm really grateful for everything you've done, Bob," he said. "However, there's no point in your hanging on here any longer. I've written to my parents, telling them to expect you, so you can make your own way home and I'll follow when I'm ready."

He handed me a purse containing my wages and sufficient to pay for my passage and that of the horses to England, then we shook hands and I left to break up my little camp in the forest. The journey to Ostend was a sad one, for the last time I had passed this way was with the troop and its magnificent horses and shining guns. I wondered how Sergeant Bambridge, Bill and the rest of them were getting on, encamped with the army near Paris.

At Ostend the horses were slung aboard a cross-channel trader, Horace protesting as usual at the indignity, and I purchased a modest berth for myself. Thanks to a good wind and tide we reached Dover later the same day. I had a longer journey back than that I had made to Colchester and Harwich. I did not mind, for although I had not been away for very long, it seemed like years since I had left home, and it was a pleasure to pass through the smiling summer landscape with its ordered villages, and to exchange greetings with friendly English faces.

It was the afternoon of 30th August when I trotted up the drive to Danesford Hall. As I turned the last bend I stopped, just as I had seen the Captain do on his return from Spain, for it was a beautiful sight, lying there in the sunlight with smoke curling from the kitchen chimney, and I realized I did not want to leave it again. My family rushed up as I clattered into the cobbled yard, all talking at once. I was shaken by the hand, slapped on the back, hugged, told I looked older, taller, thinner and needed feeding. Just then, Mrs Mason came running from the kitchen. She gave me a mighty squeeze and said that Sir Desmond and Lady Augusta wanted to see me right away, and that I was to go to the library at once.

Leaving Father to bed down Horace and Virgil, I climbed the back stairs, knocked on the library door and was bidden to enter. Sir Desmond and Lady Augusta were having tea. Sir Desmond came to meet me, smiling broadly, shook my hand and bade me sit down. This was a rare honour and even rarer was the experience of Lady Augusta pouring me tea while I was plied with cake by Miss Caroline and Miss Sophia. They had received the Captain's letter, from which they learned how I had got him to hospital and prevented the roughs from murdering him, for which they expressed their sincere gratitude. They asked me about the Captain's health when I last saw him, and everything about the battle, and laughed heartily when I told them I had spoken with Napoleon and the Duke on the same day, showing them the pass signed by Marshal Soult.

We must have been talking for half an hour when the door opened. A dark-haired lady with a statuesque figure, beautiful in a painted sort of way, entered the room and draped herself on a chaise longue.

"Ah, Bob, this is Signora Carlotta di Varenna," said Sir Desmond as I stood up.

"Your servant, ma'am," I said. I suddenly realized that I had seen her somewhere before.

She made no reply but regarded me with a half-smile, raising one eyebrow. I was conscious that a man had also come into the room.

"Roger, this is Tom Jenkins's boy, Bob," said Lady Augusta. "He was at Waterloo with Ralph and it's thanks to him that your brother is still alive."

With a shock I realized that he was the same man I had seen in Brussels. He had looked familiar because, beneath the moustache, he had the same face as the Captain, although the eyes were set closer together. He shook my hand warmly, but above the broad smile his eyes were as cold and expressionless as the huge stone holding his cravat in place.

"Then we owe you a great deal," he said. "The odd thing is, although my brother and I were in Brussels at the same time, we never bumped into each other. Now isn't that strange?"

There was a hint of menace in his words and I sensed that he was trying to discover how much I knew.

"Yes, sir, it is," I replied.

His manner became affable. "Tell you what, Bob, why don't you and I take a ride tomorrow morning, say at ten o' clock," he said. "I've not been home for a long time myself, so you can show me around and tell me about the battle – what d'you say?"

"Very good, sir," I replied, and obtained Sir Desmond's permission to leave.

Downstairs in the kitchen, I had to recite my adventures again, but I was careful to omit any mention of the Captain's brother – Mr Roger Holder. At length everyone returned to their work save for my

129

parents and Mrs Mason, who was kneading dough for the morning's bread.

"And what do you think of the Signora?" asked Mrs Mason.

"She's a fine-looking lady," I replied.

"Ha! Lady is it?" she retorted, slamming a large lump of dough on the table. "I don't think so. Signora – that means she's married, doesn't it? Well, where's her husband? That's what I'd like to know. Spends her time lying about in that finery Mr Roger buys her, flaunting her charms at every man who comes to the house! Can't think why her Ladyship has taken to her. Maybe she reminds her of herself when she was young. And, of course, Mr Roger was always her favourite, just as Captain Ralph was Sir Desmond's."

At ten o' clock the next morning I rode out with Mr Roger. He was friendly enough, but I was careful not to give a hint of my suspicions. He saw me looking curiously at the jewel in his cravat, which was almost the size of a pigeon's egg and gave off curious coloured lights from inside.

"It's an opal, Bob," he said. "I'll tell you how I came by it. Australia is an enormous country, but there's not a lot to amuse a fellow, so after I'd got the sheep farm running at a profit I decided to explore a bit. Had some camels brought in from India, because there's a lot of desert in the interior. The people who've always lived there are called Aborigines and they are very simple folk. Had a few of them working on the farm. Took one of them, whom we called Mike, along with me, because he speaks a mite of English. Well, one day, far into the outback, we came across a crowd of his people beating the daylight out of a young feller near a billabong – that is, a water hole. I fired a shot over them and they ran off. Mike said that the young feller, whom I named Sam, had offended against some tribal custom and was now an outcast – a bit like me, I suppose."

"Was he all right?" I asked.

"Yes, I patched him up and he was grateful. Mike said that in return Sam was going to take us to what he called the Place of Magic Stones. It was a couple of days' ride away, but it was worth it. That's where I found this, and many more like it, just lying on the surface. To cut a long story short, next time I was in Sydney I offered some to a Dutch merchant from Sumatra. He gave me a price that surprised me. It seemed to me that if they were worth that much out there, then they'd be worth much more in Europe. So, I went back and scooped up two or three sackfuls, then took the next ship to India."

"How did you come to be in Brussels, sir? Were you on your way home?"

"Not exactly." He laughed. "Only a fool wants to spend months at sea going round the Cape of Good Hope. From India I took a passage up the Red Sea to Egypt, and from there I sailed to Naples in Italy. It's a nice enough, free-and-easy sort of place, and it's where I met the Signora. However, Paris is rather more to my taste, so when Napoleon abdicated for the first time we moved there. Then, up he pops again, so we made ourselves scarce and went to Brussels. Thanks to the opals, I had become a wealthy man, although at the rate the Signora is spending my money I shall have to make another trip to Australia soon!"

We then talked about the battle for a while.

"I'm told you prevented my brother from being murdered while he was in hospital," he said with apparent concern.

"I happened to come in at the right moment, sir," I said guardedly. "The orderlies told me that the criminals in Brussels would rob our wounded men whenever they got the chance, even if meant killing them."

"Yes, I can imagine that," he replied, eyeing me speculatively. "I gather the ruffians responsible escaped.

Didn't recognize either of them, by any chance, did you? If you did, then we should send their description to the authorities in Brussels, because I'd dearly love to see the pair of them brought to justice."

"No, sir, it was all over very quickly."

"Luck of the devil," he said to himself, and he could have meant anything by that. "Well, Bob, it looks as though you and I are going to become good friends."

I doubted that because I did not trust him. I could not confide my suspicions to anyone because I had not the slightest proof of his involvement in the Brussels incident, yet I was filled with foreboding that something dreadful would happen when the Captain returned.

Captain Holder returned home in the middle of September, greeting me like an old friend rather than a servant. Mrs Mason said he looked thin and pale, but she had not seen him at his worst. Somehow, word had spread throughout the village that I was a hero and had saved the Captain's life. When I tried to explain that I had been scared witless until I managed to suppress my fear, and that anyone would have done the same for the Captain, those in the Dog and Duck said I shouldn't be so modest and plied me with more ale than was good for me.

Sir Desmond gave a ball to celebrate the victory and the return of all his sons, for Mr Tobias, the youngest, had completed his studies at Oxford and was on the point of joining a firm of lawyers in London. The ball, at which I was required to assist, was a great success. All the county's most eligible young ladies fluttered round the Captain, while, to the disgust of Miss Caroline and Miss Sophia, all the young gentlemen swarmed like honeybees round the

Signora. I had wondered how the Captain would get on with Mr Roger, but so far as I could see, there was nothing amiss between them.

Early in November, a shooting party was arranged. Father and I were serving mulled wine to those who had assembled when two riders jogged up the drive towards us. They were wearing a sort of uniform that included scarlet waistcoats and Father recognized them immediately.

"Redbreasts!" he exclaimed. "It's Mr Robinson and Mr Charnley, the Bow Street Runners who investigated the murder in Jackdaw Wood."

The two Runners, middle-aged men with greying hair, had expressionless faces, although their watchful eyes searched through the shooting party. They dismounted and bowed to Sir Desmond and Lady Augusta, taking off their hats as they did so.

"Good day to you, Sir Desmond, and our best respects to you, milady," said one. "No doubt you will remember us. I am Mr Robinson and this is Mr Charnley. You engaged us some years ago to investigate a local murder."

"Ah, and here's Captain Ralph Holder, returned safely from the wars, I'm glad to see," said Mr Charnley. "And Mr Roger Holder, recently returned from Australia, we understand. Good day to you both, gentlemen."

"What brings you back here?" asked Sir Desmond. "I thought our business was finished."

"No, sir, it was not," replied Mr Robinson. "You'll remember I told you we never close our files on a case of murder. Well, now we believe we have solved that case, do we not, Mr Charnley?"

"Indeed we do, Mr Robinson. We are here to make an arrest, Sir Desmond, and while we regret that this will cause you and her ladyship much grief, yet it will please you that we can also clear the name of an innocent and honourable man."

"Roger Holder," said Mr Robinson sharply, "I am arresting you on the grounds that on or about the night of 3rd January in the year of our Lord 1800, you did wilfully murder one Amos Wykes, also known as Smiler Wykes, at Marsh Farm, Danesford, in the county of Loamshire. You are further charged that you sought to pervert the course of justice by attempting to implicate one Ralph Holder in the said murder, knowing him to be innocent. You are not obliged to say anything, but anything you do say will be taken down and may be used in evidence against you."

There was a sudden gasp from everyone present. Lady Augusta fainted and was hurriedly taken indoors.

"And just who do you suppose is going to believe all that?" said Mr Roger, laughing. "You haven't a shred of evidence, you fool!"

"Ah, now that's where you're mistaken, Mr Roger Holder," said Mr Charnley. "We've all we need to make you swing, sir. No honour among thieves, is there, Mr Robinson?"

"Not so you'd notice, Mr Charnley, especially when it's their own necks that might be stretched. Remember Jack Higgins, Mr Holder? You knew him as Cross-Eyed Jack. Well, after he left here in something of a hurry, he went to London. Crime was all he knew, and he got in with a very unpleasant crowd."

"Very unpleasant," said Mr Charnley. "Last year they robbed a shopkeeper, beating him to a pulp. We'd had a tip-off, so some of our lads were nearby. Old Jack's not as nimble as he was and they collared him. When the shopkeeper died, the charge was raised from robbery with violence to murder. Rather than hang, Jack turned King's Evidence and served as a witness against his mates, so it was them who went for the drop. Since then, we've had many a long talk with Jack, who told us enough to clear a score of crimes off the books. That was very helpful, seeing we're both retiring from the service next year, wouldn't you say, Mr Robinson?"

"I would indeed, Mr Charnley. Told us all about your little arrangement with Smiler Wykes. You knew where all the balls and parties in the county were taking place, who would be going, what sort of jewellery they had and the route they would be taking home. Smiler would hold up their coaches and give you a cut of the proceeds. Now, according to Jack, you weren't satisfied with the size of that cut, so you arranged to meet Smiler Wykes at Jack's farm and have it out with him. There was an argument between the two of you, and it ended with you stabbing Smiler three times."

"Did I?" Roger was still smiling confidently. "What it boils down to is the word of a known criminal against mine. Which do you think a jury will accept? You can't prove a thing, so why don't the pair of you just clear off and go about your business?"

Mr Charnley returned to the attack. I thought that the way the Runners took turns at pounding Roger with facts and accusations was, in its way, as remorseless and frightening as the fire of the French guns at Waterloo.

"Well and good, if that was the case, but there's more to come. You see, Jack's crowd in London regularly used a fence – that is, a man who will buy stolen property. His name was Sigmund Kramer and he was one of the biggest in the business. Sometimes he bought in items from fences outside London – items that were too hot or too valuable for them to handle locally. Thanks to Jack, we got him and all the evidence we needed, then blow me if he didn't turn King's Evidence as well."

"Quite so," continued Mr Robinson. "We've picked up fences all round the country, including a Mr Aaron Silverman here in Dunchester. He admitted buying from Smiler Wykes, and when your little dispute arose, Smiler asked him to attend the meeting at Jack's farm and confirm that you were getting your fair share of the loot. Didn't know that, did you Mr Holder?"

"And you didn't know that Silverman arrived late, did you?" added Mr Charnley. "Or that he was looking through the window at the moment you stabbed Smiler? Or that he watched you and Jack carry the body into Jackdaw Wood? Well, both he and Jack are

139

willing to give evidence now. What do you say to that, Mr Roger Holder?

"It's a pack of lies!" snarled Roger.

"No, sir, it is not," said Mr Robinson. "But then it wasn't really Smiler you were after. You were after bigger game. You wanted your brother to hang for the murder, then you would be next in line to inherit the estate, and be able to pay off your debts. Is that not so?"

"We knew as soon as we saw the evidence you planted," said Mr Charnley. "It was too obvious. Very amateur, if I may say so. Your brother had no reason at all to kill Smiler, and you seemed to have forgotten that. Now, sir, we both know that you are going to hang, so why not make a clean breast of it?"

Sir Desmond had gone ashen and Father was supporting him as he seemed to be on the point of collapse. The Captain walked over to his brother who was stroking his moustache and staring into space.

"You must have hated me," he said. "Why? What have I ever done to you?"

"I didn't hate you while we were boys, old fellow," replied Roger, his old charming self again. "None of it mattered then. Later, I came to hate you because you are an hour older than I am, because that made you the heir, because you came first in everything, because it was you everyone wanted their daughters to marry. But mostly I hated you because we were both brought up to be country gentlemen, and while you would continue to be one, I would have to go out into the world and grub a living."

"You could have made a good life for yourself in Australia," said the Captain, but his brother ignored him.

"You may as well know, I hired a couple of buckos to finish you off while you were in hospital. Told me they'd done it, too, otherwise I'd never have come home." He turned and pointed at me. "It now seems that before they could finish the job they were set on by this lad of yours, damn him."

"Time we were on our way, sir," said Mr Robinson, pulling a set of manacles from his pocket.

"I say, old chap, d'you mind if I visit the yard privy first?" asked Roger, smiling broadly. "It would be darn difficult for me with the bracelets on, what!"

They followed him across the yard and stood outside when he closed the door. Suddenly, from inside, came the sound of a shot. We all ran over as the two Runners wrenched open the bolted door. Roger lay face down, a cloud of powder smoke hanging over him. Mr Robinson turned him over, revealing a large wound in his chest. It was obvious that he was dead. Mr Charnley picked up a small pocket pistol that had been lying under the body.

"Kept it hidden inside his fancy waistcoat, no doubt," he said.

"Loaded with a full charge of buckshot," commented Mr Robinson, as he stood up after examining the wound. "No ball would have made a mess like that."

He turned to the Captain. "Now why would a man want a pocket pistol charged with buckshot when he's going out for a day's shooting with friends?" he said. "People get shot by accident, of course, and it's my belief that you could have suffered such a misfortune in an hour or two, sir. They say the Almighty works in mysterious ways."

Mr Charnley pulled a leather pouch from Roger's coat pocket and emptied three polished opals into the palm of his hand. I guessed that these were all that were left.

"Opals – there's some say they bring bad luck," he said. "Maybe they do and maybe they don't. They don't seem to have done him much good, anyway."

Epilogue

June 1817

That, then is my story of Waterloo, the battle that has finally brought peace to Europe, and the solving of the Smiler Wykes murder mystery. Lady Augusta has never really recovered from the tragedy, and nor has Sir Desmond. Captain Holder has left the Army to take over the running of the estate. Mrs Mason was upset for weeks, blaming Signora di Varenna for Mr Roger's death.

The Signora was given enough money to pay for her return to Naples, although Mrs Mason says she would probably get no further than London before she found another beau to look after her. Sergeant Nathan Bambridge, having taken his discharge, has returned to take up his duties as under-gamekeeper and has married Polly Partridge.

Others from the troop have been to see us. Captain Burnham, as he is now, has stayed in the Army and commands his own troop. Mr Holt will not be too handicapped by the loss of his hand, for he is a teacher of mathematics at a boys' school and when his pension is added to his salary he says he can live comfortably. Mr Elliot has returned to his family's estate in Ireland. Bill Grover, who had also taken his discharge, made a special journey to say goodbye to us, for he had made up his mind to leave the country.

"The fact is, Bob, I shall starve if I stay here," he said. "As you know, there are thousands of us discharged soldiers and seamen looking for work, and there's none to be had, save for a pittance. Anyway, the Spanish colonies in South America are fighting for their freedom from Spain, and they are recruiting British soldiers, whom they know they can trust. Well, soldiering is all I know, the wages are good and I've picked up a bit of the lingo, so it seems the obvious thing to do."

The Captain gave him ten pounds and wished him a safe return to better times.

As for myself, the Captain had been told I'd handled the teams well at Waterloo and that has led to my present position: learning the duties of a coachman. I am told that in a year or two I am to replace Sir Desmond's second coachman, Harry Chambers, who is now getting old and unable to sit on the box in all weathers without becoming ill.

I had thought that Horace and Virgil would be sold, but it was decided to keep them on as veterans of the great battle who had served us well.

One day last year the Captain came into the tack room, where I was polishing the brasses on the harness.

"You'll be pleased to learn that the Government has awarded prize money for Waterloo," he said. "I've collected yours for you and here it is – two pounds, eleven shillings and four pence."

"Thank you, sir, but I was not a soldier there," I replied, startled and pleased by this windfall.

"Oh, didn't I tell you?" he said. "Well, as you did as much as any and more than some, I had you entered on the troop roll as a volunteer driver. And one other thing – the Government has also given each of us a medal."

He reached into his pocket and handed me mine. It was a beautiful thing, hanging from a crimson ribbon with blue borders. On one side was a figure I was told represented the Winged Victory holding an olive branch, together with the words WELLINGTON and WATERLOO 18th JUNE 1815, and on the other, was a portrait of the Prince Regent wearing a laurel wreath.

"Should this not be the King's portrait, as we have on our coins, sir?" I asked in surprise.

"Ah, well, the Prince Regent has been telling people he was there. Did you see him, Bob?"

"No, sir, I did not."

"Nor did I. Nor did anyone else. I dare say that now it's all over we'll be meeting lots of people who'll tell us they were there!" At this we both laughed heartily.

So, here I sit now, reminiscing. On the table in front of me I have three souvenirs – the pass that the Emperor Napoleon ordered Marshal Soult to give me, the *Medaille Militaire* belonging to Sergeant François Dumas of the Grenadiers of the Old Guard, and my own Waterloo Medal. Little things, perhaps, but reminders of the day on which I saw history made.

Historical note

Once he had regained his throne, Napoleon realised immediately that the European Powers would mobilise their armies against him. He perceived, correctly, that the greatest threat was posed by two Allied armies in the Low Countries, known today as Holland and Belgium, which could easily strike into northern France. Leaving small armies to protect France's frontiers with Spain, Italy and along the Rhine, he concentrated his best troops in the Army of the North and advanced into Belgium, planning to defeat each of the Allied armies in turn.

Having defeated Marshal Blucher's Prussian army at the Battle of Ligny on 16 June 1815, Napoleon despatched Marshal Emmanuel de Grouchy in pursuit with 40,000 men and 104 guns. Grouchy mistakenly thought that the Prussians were retreating eastwards towards Germany when they were actually withdrawing northwards to Wavre in order to stay in contact with the Duke of Wellington's Allied army. Consequently, he did not catch up with them in sufficient numbers to prevent the main body of their army cooperating with Wellington two days later.

Wellington, who had fought a successful delaying action at Quatre Bras on 16 June, withdrew to the Waterloo position the following day to conform with the Prussian movement. His army consisted of 50,000 infantry, 12,500 cavalry and 156 guns, a total of 68,000 men. Of these, one-third were British, only a small proportion of whom were the magnificent troops with whom he had won the Peninsula War in Spain and Portugal, the rest being Dutch-Belgian or German allies. One Royal Horse Artillery troop was partially equipped with rockets, which had entered service with the British Army two years earlier, and Bob witnessed these in action during the final stages of the withdrawal from Quatre Bras.

Napoleon deployed 49,000 infantry, 15,750 cavalry and 246 guns. Because hours of torrential rain had so softened the ground as to reduce the efficiency of his artillery, he was not able to commence his assault on Wellington's position until late on the morning of 18 June. He began by ordering Lieutenant General Count Reille's II Corps to attack the chateau of Hougoumont. This was intended as a distraction designed to induce Wellington to reinforce his right wing in strength by taking units from his centre, against which the principal attack was to be launched. The Duke, however, declined to do this and, meeting the most determined resistance imaginable, Reille allowed his entire corps to be sucked into a battle within a battle that was to last the entire day.

At about 1.30 p.m., Lieutenant General Drouet d'Erlon's I Corps launched its attack, the intention being to take the farm of La Haye Sainte, lying in advance of Wellington's position, and smash through the left-centre of the Allied line. La Haye Sainte held out, the French were halted by the steady fire of British infantry and then charged by the Household and Union heavy cavalry brigades. D'Erlon's corps, decimated, became a mob of fugitives, with several thousand of its men being taken prisoner. Unfortunately, some of the British cavalry charged too far, and although they managed to reach Napoleon's Grand Battery of guns, where they cut down the gunners, they themselves were cut down when the French cavalry counter-charged. Nevertheless, Napoleon's plan for the battle had failed.

At about this time a captured despatch informed Napoleon that the Prussians were marching towards him from the east. He promptly ordered Lieutenant General Count Lobau's VI Corps to form a defensive front facing in that direction, based on the village of

Plancenoit. All three of his infantry corps had now been committed to the battle. D'Erlon managed to rally some of his troops and continue the attacks on La Haye Sainte.

Feeling unwell, Napoleon left the field for a while, leaving the conduct of the battle to Marshal Michel Ney. To protect his infantry from the fire of the French guns, Wellington ordered them to retire behind the crest of the Mont St Jean ridge. Observing this, the movement of empty ammunition wagons, wounded men and what were actually columns of French prisoners being marched to the rear, Ney mistakenly concluded that the Allied army was withdrawing. He immediately launched a mass attack with his cavalry.

The British gunners fired into the advancing mass until the last possible moment, then ran for cover to the nearest infantry squares. Shot down in droves, the French were unable to penetrate the bayonets of the squares and were then driven off by the Allied cavalry. At this point the gunners returned to their guns and fired into the backs of the retreating enemy. During the afternoon, this was repeated a dozen or so times until the French cavalry had been virtually destroyed. A saying later arose that if they had brought with them a bag of nails with which to spike the touchholes of the

British guns, the outcome of the battle might have been different, but this is open to debate.

Napoleon was furious with Ney for having wasted his magnificent cavalry. As the Prussians were becoming heavily involved with Lobau's corps in and around Plancenoit, he spread the deliberate lie among the troops facing the Allied army that the guns they could hear to the east belonged to Grouchy, who was about to fall on Wellington's left flank, when actually it was his own right flank that was coming under pressure.

During the early evening the small but heroic Allied garrison of La Haye Sainte ran out of ammunition and the farm finally fell to the French. A number of Dutch-Belgian and German units in the vicinity promptly fled, leaving a huge gap in the centre of Wellington's line. Ney lacked both infantry and cavalry with which to exploit the situation, and by the time Napoleon sanctioned the use of the Imperial Guard, Wellington had closed the gap, using units drawn from his flanks.

The attack of Guard was met by the British Foot Guards in one of the most famous encounters of the Napoleonic Wars. As Bob describes in his story, a Dutch battery also fired into one flank of the French columns, while the British 52nd Regiment wheeled to its left out of the main line and raked the other with its fire. The

Guard had always been victorious and when it broke in headlong flight, the French army fell apart and took to its heels in a panic-stricken rout, pursued without mercy by the Prussian cavalry. Several battalions of the Old Guard fought to the death and the remnant of the Guard cavalry hurried Napoleon off the field.

Napoleon reached Paris on 21 June and abdicated the following day.

Wellington's army sustained the loss of 15,000 men killed and wounded, of whom 9,999 were British. The Prussians lost approximately 7,000 killed and wounded. The French Army of the North was all but destroyed, 25,000 of its men being killed or wounded, 8,000 taken prisoner and 220 of its guns captured.

The battle had been fought in a comparatively small area measuring approximately two-and-a-half miles by one mile. Within this space lay 47,000 dead or wounded men and no less than 25,000 horses. It took weeks to clear the field, the last of the living wounded being found 15 days after the battle.

The Battle of Waterloo ensured that the great powers of Europe would remain at peace with each other for the next forty years. In the United Kingdom, the government drastically reduced the size of the Army and the Royal Navy, with the result that many thousands of former soldiers and seamen found themselves without work. Some emigrated to Canada, South Africa, Australia or the United States. Others, like Bob's friend, Bill Grover, joined the rebels in Spain's Central and South American colonies, who were fighting for their independence from the mother country. In the new countries that were founded, their contribution is honoured to this day. Their presence led to a new word being coined. They continued to sing the marching songs they had used in Spain under Wellington, notably "Green Grow the Rushes, O!". To local ears, this sounded like *gringo*, a term later used to describe anyone of Anglo-Saxon descent, including Americans.

Picture acknowledgements

P156   Plan of the Battle of Waterloo, András Bereznay
P157   Napoleon I, Mary Evans Picture Library/Douglas McCarthy
P158   The Duke of Wellington at Waterloo by Robert Alexander Hillingford (Private Collection), Christie's Images/Bridgeman Art Library
P159   Waterloo, Mary Evans Picture Library/Douglas McCarthy
P160   Waterloo Campaign Medal, author's own collection

Timeline

6 April 1814 The Emperor Napoleon Bonaparte, defeated in France by the Allied armies, abdicates and is confined to the island of Elba, off the Italian coast. King Louis XVIII is restored to the throne of France.

26 February 1815 Napoleon escapes from Elba.

1 March Napoleon lands in France and commences his march on Paris.

20 March Napoleon reaches Paris, from which Louis XVIII has already fled to Belgium.

April – Early June Allies mobilize for war. Austrian and Russian armies begin assembling on the River Rhine in Germany. A Prussian army under Marshal Prince Blucher enters Belgium, where an Anglo-Dutch-German army is being assembled under the Duke of Wellington. Wellington and Blucher agree to cooperate.

15 June Napoleon crosses the Belgian frontier at the head of the French army of the North.

16 June Defeated at the Battle of Ligny, the Prussians withdraw northwards to Wavre. Wellington's army fights a successful delaying action at Quatre Bras.

17 June To conform with the Prussians, Wellington's army withdraws to Mont St Jean, just south of Waterloo.

18 June The Battle of Waterloo.

Morning The French attack Hougoumont chateau, where fighting continues throughout the day.

Afternoon The French attack on the centre-left of Wellington's line defeated with heavy losses, although serious casualties are sustained by the British heavy cavalry. Massed French cavalry attacks on the centre of Wellington's line are repulsed. The Prussians begin entering the battle from the east. The French finally capture the farm of La Haye Sainte.

Evening The attack by the Imperial Guard on Wellington's centre is repulsed. The French army disintegrates in flight and is pursued by Blucher's Prussians.

22 June Napoleon abdicates for the second time.

15 July Napoleon surrenders himself to the British, boarding HMS *Bellerophon* at the Ile d'Aix.

7 August Napoleon sails aboard HMS *Northumberland* for lifelong exile on the island of St Helena.

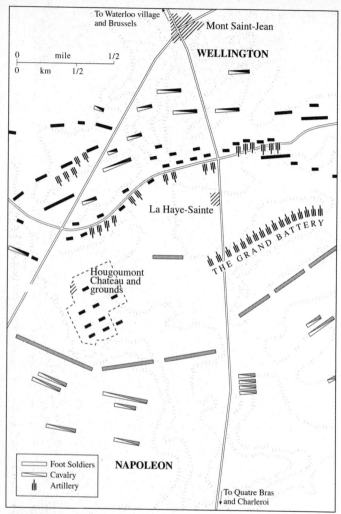

A plan of the Battle of Waterloo with the positions of Napoleon's French army and Wellington's Allied army.

Napoleon Bonaparte on his grey horse, surrounded by his Marshals.

The Royal Horse Artillery fire a 6-pounder gun at the attacking French (left), while the Duke of Wellington encourages the infantry.

British soldiers form a square and defend themselves for five hours against French cavalry attacks.

The Waterloo campaign medal – showing Winged Victory and, on the reverse, the Prince Regent (later King George IV) who claimed to be at the battle.